I'LL DO ANYTHING YOU WANT

IOLANDA BATALLÉ

I'LL DO ANYTHING YOU WANT

Translated from Catalan by
Maruxa Relaño and Martha Tennent

3TimesRebel

First published by 3TimesRebel Press in 2023, our second year of existence.

Title: *I'll Do Anything You Want* by Iolanda Batallé

Original title: *Faré tot el que tu vulguis*
Copyright © Iolanda Batallé Prats, 2013
c/o Ute Körner Literary Agent

Originally published by Edicions 62, S.A.

Translation from Catalan: Copyright © Maruxa Relaño and Martha Tennent, 2023

Design and layout: Enric Jardí

Illustrations: Anna Pont Armengol

Editing and proof reading: Greg Mulhern, Carme Bou, Bibiana Mas

Maria-Mercè Marçal's poem *Deriva*:
© heiresses of Maria-Mercè Marçal

Translation of Maria-Mercè Marçal's poem *Deriva*:
© Dr Sam Abrams

Author photograph: © Francesc Orteu

The translation of this book is supported by Institut Ramon Llull.

 institut
ramon llull

Printed and bound by TJ Books, Padstow, Cornwall, England
Paperback ISBN: 978-1-7398236-2-7
eBook ISBN: 978-1-7391287-3-9 / 978-1-7398236-7-2

www.3timesrebel.com

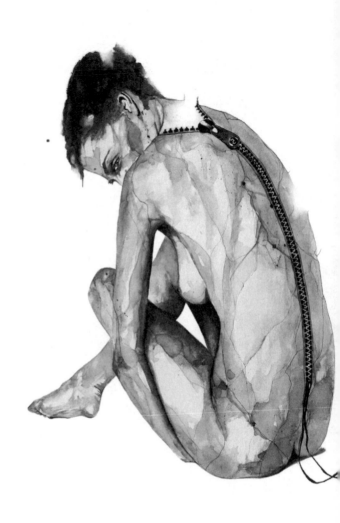

BEFORE THE MEN ARRIVED AND BUILT THE ROAD TO THAT remote area, loneliness had made the women of the village fling themselves into the sea. Happy, their long hair flowing. The flight attendant reminded them to buckle up, they were about to land. Once their seatbelts were fastened, he whispered that, with everyone secure in their seats, no one would see them. The legend of the women with long hair and smiling eyes—it was a story she'd heard from her grandfather when she was a child. The plane was half empty.

His name was Nacho, they'd met at the airport, and now he was pinching her nipple, hard. For twenty-five years she'd been a faithful wife. He stroked her knees, and when his right hand slipped beneath her skirt, he discovered that Nora was wearing a garter belt. Some of the men who arrived in the village went mad, others married local girls. Before the strangers opened up the road, loneliness had driven the women to cast themselves into the sea. For weeks, Nora would remember the white headrest of the seat in front of her with British Airways printed on it in blue letters. And the pain in her nipples, while she bit down on his hand. She would also remember the words of the taxi driver who drove her to Heathrow. My name is Paul Smith Page, but only one of my surnames is real.

Nacho was a strange mix of containment and lust. Nora didn't know what to expect, and it aroused her. The flight attendant's head reappeared, she was chasing a can of Coca-Cola that was rolling down the aisle. Nora straightened up. The stewardess smiled at them (she'd tackled the can) and returned to her seat. A bit on edge, lest the air hostess return, Nora continued to pleasure him with her right hand. He bit her nipples until they hurt. Dying from a gunshot wound had to be terrible, but death by a spear gun while swimming in the sea was the worst thing she could imagine. She was about to climax. Her first orgasm outside her marriage. She didn't feel guilty. The plane landed but he continued to squeeze her. Nothing would ever be the same; the thought of no one ever touching her like that again was unbearable. She remembered the ankles of the man who drove her to the airport. Sure you're not running late? the taxi driver had said. Something about him reminded her of Alice's white rabbit.

The sound of the sea transports us to a remote past. The hum of the waves and the smell of salt water are ensconced in the most primitive regions of our brain, the parts that control our breathing and movement. To return to the sea is to return home. We do as turtles do: our species retreats back to the water. Mammals are descended from a small, furry dinosaur that outlived the others. Whales and dolphins share a common ancestor with the cow, the dolphin being the result of the species' ability to halt evolution at a certain point in time. Nacho had talked about these things after asking her if she had an inward or outward gaze. He confessed he had a secret.

The memory-hued sound and smell of the sea resides in the most primitive regions of our brain. There was one week in December when she swam every day; she was sad and the sea, the gelid water, seemed to cleanse everything. It was sunny that week. Her head throbbed after diving in, but after a few minutes her body grew accustomed to the cold. She felt brave: never again would she need anyone. When you enter the sea at Cala dels Corbs in December, your breathing quickens, you dive underwater and, when your head and body reappear you don't feel cold anymore, you actually feel warm. You stretch out your fingers and arms, you feel invincible, your breasts firm. That was the sensation that most resembled her experience on the plane. That December she walked down to the sea, removed her clothes, left them folded by her straw basket, and dived in the water. She always emerged feeling strong, confident, pretty. She wrapped her hair in one towel, her body in another, and sat by the water's edge and breathed. The sea heals everything. So does resolve. And, what was she doing now? That man had shrouded her brain like a colicky baby, swathed from head to toe. She had seen a video of one when the girls were little. The idea was to ease the babies' discomfort: the fabric simulated the mother's uterus, it helped them relax and shielded them from the harshness of their new world. She quickly opened her handbag, reached for the piece of rubber and sniffed it.

One January morning, some men came and pruned the five plane trees on the promenade in front of her beach apartment. They pruned two of them, a tall strong tree with a massive trunk, and a smaller one, young but also strong, that stood next to it. They cut down the remaining three, leaving only the stumps. She watched from the terrace: the strong one with the massive trunk was her grandfather, she was the small one, young and strong, the other three were her parents and her grandmother. On that winter morning Nora lost more than those three trees. She crossed the promenade and walked over to them. Of the felled trees only the stumps remained, about thirty centimetres high. She moved closer and touched them, the wood was dry and warm and had a distinct smell. One was rotten, with a black circle in the middle. She stuck her finger in, it was soft and humid, and made a sound like someone stepping in a puddle. A dark brown worm, a resident of the tree, inched up her hand, leaving a trail of tepid slime. Yes, one of the tree trunks was rotten, that's why it had been cut, but what about the other two? She sniffed the piece of rubber and walked up the aisle to exit the plane. Nacho was watching her.

THE COST OF LIVING KEEPS RISING, AND YET HUMANKIND HAS recently gone down in value. Nora strode along the jetway without looking back. She knew he was watching. His gaze held a deep nostalgia, a feeling so tangible, so solid she could almost knead it, the way she did when she had baked with her grandmother. Nacho watched her, her black skirt just above the knee, her blazer, her swaying hips. He noted with amusement that the men desired her and even the women were looking at her. He'd always wanted to know what had happened to his mother, but he'd never found a single clue. His mother had turned blue after being with a man who was not his father. Dead. He'd witnessed it by chance, he was supposed to be at school. Mother's turned blue! There's nothing that can be done. That's when he decided to become a shark. Seven years later he heard the song *King of Pain* for the first time. Each new woman he met held the promise of discovering the key to that mystery. This one reminded him of the ballerina in the music box he had as a child.

He was the king of pain. It was his shield, if you're the king you're immune to hurt. But it had been a while since he'd felt like a king. She was almost unattractive in her beauty. The woman had bumps on her head, he mentioned it when he stroked it. She laughed because no one had ever mentioned it before. Nora liked her bumpy head. She remembered a scene she'd witnessed from the terrace of her beach flat: two small black dogs with shaggy fur like a curtain. Two black curtains trotting along, performing a sort of comedy routine on the dirt path by the sea. Behind the dogs walks a man with his hands clasped behind his back. Ahead of them is a young woman with long, curly black hair wearing a red leather miniskirt. She's walking fast, she has both dogs on the same leash, and every now and then she stops to wait and glances back at them. Suddenly, she opens her black silk blouse and exposes two enormous breasts, which she takes in her hands. The man stops and pinches her nipples. She bears it and breathes deeply, her face assumes a smile. They continue like that for half a minute; one of the dogs relieves himself on a rock, the other sniffs the urine. The young woman buttons her blouse again and they go on their way. There was no one left by the baggage carousel. Not a soul. Just a black suitcase and a silver one.

'Would you do that again?' Nacho said after she'd retrieved the silver suitcase.

'Do what?'

'Bend over like that, so your hands touch the floor.'

Nora turned around and crouched, and Nacho watched her. He snapped a photo of her. I suspect it's been too long since a man took your picture. Robert used to when they were first together, but not anymore. It had been a while since her husband—the dignified and fair-minded Senyor Attorney, founder of what had once been one of the more prestigious law firms in town, the man who kissed her on the forehead every morning as he left for work—had taken an interest in the inner workings of his wife's heart. When you stop probing your husband's silences for hidden treasure, you're in trouble. Neither of them made an effort. The man bored her. There were moments when, despite the love she still felt for him, she found him repulsive. She no longer liked his touch. And the problems at his law firm, which was now struggling, were of no interest to her. Family and married life can make a couple invisible to one another. She'd found herself missing her daughters, and had phoned them from London: but Mamà, you only left yesterday! her youngest daughter said. The heart is a lonely hunter, no doubt about it. And Cloe had been pedalling towards her own independence for quite a while now. Nora was proud of her daughters' independence. She'd raised them that way. But now she felt lost, she needed something more. She was searching for something she had yet to find. She was an artist. She should be preparing her new show, but for the first time, sublimating her emptiness into art wasn't enough. She needed two strong arms to hold her. Robert held her, yes, but always in the same way, with the same intensity, and after so many years together she was inured to his touch. It bored her. Nora lived where everyone with a family lives, on the edge of an abyss.

She let him take more photos.

'I'll give you a lift home.'

'No. I'll take a taxi.'

'I'll be glad to.'

'I've already told you, I have a family.'

'I have a dog. Not a problem. Don't worry, I won't lay a finger on you in the car.'

She accepted. It was surreal to discover that the idea of being without him was suddenly unbearable. After shagging him she'd end it. She was in charge, she'd never depended on anyone, but she didn't want to suffer either. Nacho had just said he wouldn't touch her. But she wanted him to touch her. There was nothing wrong with that. Some men cut down trees, they leave behind only the rotten trunk, the slimy worm. Seagulls, there were more of them every day.

Seagulls had been taking over the city for some time: just the other day she'd watched them pecking away at sandwiches in the playground of the school in front of her house. Her own daughters had attended that school and had been able to enjoy their snacks in peace, without being terrorised by birds. Now the teachers were at their wits' end. And you're sure you're not running late? That's what the taxi driver would have said if he'd been Alice's White Rabbit. All she could think of were the seagulls. It's the only way of making contact with a dinosaur, she told herself, recalling the two couples she'd seen feeding a gull on the beach. All birds are dinosaurs, her grandfather used to say. A plucked seagull is a chicken. Days before, on the beach, she'd watched two Czech couples giving water to one of the birds. Nora thought they could make a gull-dog out of it, man's best friend, put a string around its neck and walk it through town. Maybe the bird wanted to migrate north and didn't know how. Seagulls would be the end of us. While the Czechs were busy offering water to the seagull, a woman from the village complained: that's all we need, foreigners coming and feeding the birds!

COME HERE A SECOND, I CAN'T LET YOU LEAVE LIKE THIS. HE kissed her on the lips and gave her a small fabric-covered black box. For you. Open it! She'd asked him to stop the car, she wanted to get out. She'd realised she didn't want to arrive home with a stranger. Inside the box were two gold earrings in the shape of a double-leaf, a diamond in the centre of each leaf.

'From an antique dealer in Segovia, a shop called Cambalache. The lady who runs the place told me they were made in the early nineteenth century, for the countess, a woman of rare beauty. No one has worn them since she died. Try them on!'

He gave her one of his Bogart grins. It was cold out.

'They're beautiful, but … I can't …'

'Just try them on. I'd love to see them on you. They say when the countess wore them men fell at her feet.'

'What did the countess die of?'

'A man swore his undying love for her.'

'Sorry?'

'In love there should be no promises.'

'I don't get it.'

'Exactly that. Promises weigh heavily on love. No love can withstand too many vows and promises. Is love real because one loves, or because of a promise?' Nacho didn't wait for a reply. 'The countess married a strong, beautiful man who pledged his eternal love for her, but the promise doomed them. She suspected him of seeing other women, of loving her only because of his vow. Even though it wasn't true, she died of heartbreak. Her heart simply gave out. I didn't know that could even happen, but apparently it's true, the antiquarian told me ... You can't take them off. They're yours! You're the countess now.'

Nora had begun to weep. Nacho hugged her and his face was covered with her tears. We're not promising each other eternal love. His index finger drew circles on the palm of her hand. Nora wept even more. Don't cry, the bit about the Countess of Segovia isn't even true. It's just a myth. A heart that dies from love! Nora knew it was true though: hearts do shatter. A broken heart is something real.

'I know you'll call me.'

She accepted the earrings.

'I will not. And what of him?' What she did or didn't do seemed to have little effect on Nacho.

'Who?'

'The beautiful man who pledged his undying love.'

'They say he killed himself by jumping from the aqueduct.'

She slammed the car door shut and started walking up Balmes. The love story she'd just heard was all too familiar.

You'll phone me! She shook her head without looking back, the gold earrings glistening in her black hair. She would not. She did not want him. She would not love him. I'll give her twenty-four hours, he thought, and the uncertainty excited him. Nora walked on, counting her steps. She mustn't look back. Twenty-five, twenty-six, twenty-seven. What is happening to me? Have I ever been in love? Thirty. Who am I? Thirty-two, thirty-three. He has a freckle above his lip. I will not turn around. If you don't know who you love, you don't know who you are. I know nothing. I love Robert. The truth, always the truth. I will water the plants. It's a bit like praying, only with water. I'll do a lot of watering.

THE ALARM WENT OFF. SHE PUT HER ARMS AROUND ROBERT and snuggled up. He was still strong. She pictured the white headrest with 'British Airways' printed in blue letters and felt the soreness in her nipples. She'd chosen the white sheets with blue stripes when making the bed. You always sleep well in your own bed after being away from home.

Few things were more pleasant than that first night of sleeping on clean sheets; she'd felt that way since she was a child. She remembered all the nights her grandfather had tucked her into a freshly made bed. Later, after she was married, she would ask Robert to tuck her in like her grandfather used to, and he would. Sometimes, to this day, her daughters would ask the same of her. Even Jana, who was studying medicine now and stayed at her boyfriend's more often than she did at home.

'Argh,' Robert said. 'Alarm clocks should be banned on Sundays. Cloe's volleyball tournament better be over soon.'

'Still a few months to go ... remember the indoor play parks? All those years of birthday parties?'

'That was more than ten years ago, Nora. Now it's strictly volleyball for us.'

'That playground on Avinguda Roma, at the birthday party for one of Jana's friends, little Felix Sagristà? All the mums started dancing and singing *Tu Chica Yeyé*. Remember? The MC divided everyone into two groups: the boys were pirates and the girls were divas. The mums joined in with their daughters, they too were divine. And when *Hoy No Me Puedo Levantar* started playing they all went wild. There was one heavily pregnant woman who was dancing like a maniac, everyone was afraid she'd go into labour right there on the dance floor. I was sitting next to you. It was the kind of thing I never did. I wondered if Cloe and Jana would have preferred a mother who danced to *Tu Chica Yeyé*. A mother like the others. I even wondered if you'd have preferred a wife who was more like them.'

'What's all this nonsense?'

'Those women were having fun. The Ruined Women's Collective of Baix Llobregat, you called them. Remember? And the pregnant woman, you said she'd probably been rejected from the talent show Operación Triunfo ... How to ruin your child's life with one song ... .'

'I've always made you laugh.'

'Yes.'

'Why are you telling me this now?' Robert pulled her closer; she was crying, something she rarely did. 'You're exhausted. They've decided against your exhibition and you can't stand for your work to be passed over. Most of us slow down when we're tired. Not you.'

'They didn't take my paintings. They liked them, but said

it was too risky, what with the crisis and all. I'm washed up, I feel worthless.'

Nora realised she wasn't crying about what she was saying, but about what she was keeping to herself.

'Forget it, Nora. You're tired. New earrings?'

'Yes, from an antique shop in the Portobello Market. I think I'm going to wear them for a while. You like them?'

She surprised herself by that little lie. Suddenly, her husband plus Nacho seemed like the right combination, the way forward. A way to stare down the abyss and keep herself from falling.

'Yes, I do.'

Robert caressed her while she took in the view of the city from her bed and fantasised about the Countess of Segovia and her count, both of whom had died for love. She knew it was possible to die for love. The whole city lay before her. On their wedding night, Robert had carried her across the threshold: *amor meu*, in this fairy tale you are the princess! They always told each other that they lived in the loveliest house in Barcelona, they felt like the kings of a city that day in, day out, awoke each morning at their feet. They'd lived in the house for more than twenty years, but it had been a while since she'd looked out the window. My name is Paul Smith Page, but of the two surnames only one is real. She didn't understand why the taxi driver's words reverberated in her mind. His fleshy hands were pink, the colour of pigs before slaughter, and had white curly hairs on the back. Her grandfather used to take her with him to the annual pig slaughter—the hysterical squealing as the pig died! The idea of death made her want to live. Perhaps, only while love remains unfulfilled is it able to keep its mystery, though she'd always believed that loving and being loved in return was the best thing that could happen to anyone. Why was it no longer the case with them? Maybe the taxi driver had the answer and she hadn't known how to listen.

For many years, she'd disavowed her own suffering because she'd lived in that house, with the love of her life and their two beautiful daughters. They led a charmed life, she couldn't possibly be sad, her privilege wouldn't allow it. It had been a wedding gift from her grandfather, the house. She had no complaints. Her art was successful. She'd stopped crying now, her husband continued to stroke her face and hair. She'd never doubted Robert, she would never find herself in the Countess of Segovia's shoes. She and Robert had promised each other undying love and they had been together for twenty-five years. Were they happy? For Robert, she was the only one. She realised that love and one's fantasy of love cancelled each other out. When you start to reflect on love, love is already gone. What's left then? What those of us who have loved tend to latch onto: the deeply-held belief that we love, and always will love that person, that family, that life. Then what? Something different. Believing in love is just that, a belief, and meanwhile love itself searches for windows.

THINGS THAT APPEAR TO BE ONE THING ARE ACTUALLY NOT what they seem, they are something else entirely. Nora was finishing her coffee, before that she was barely human. Then she would go down to her studio and paint. She liked the smell of coffee. She couldn't fathom the idea that there could be people with children or careers who didn't drink coffee. She had a wall covered with quotes, one of which was from her mother, the only words of hers she remembered: *Love is free or it isn't love*. Her favourite one to read in the morning was by Oscar Wilde. *Only dull people are brilliant at breakfast.* Ever since the flight she'd felt like she belonged to someone else. To feel that her man was not the one waiting for her at home was something new to her. When I love you always means something else. She recalled the two figures she'd happened upon years ago, fused together on the breakwater. She'd been riding her bicycle, the girls were little and she'd slipped away for a while. A blond boy and a brown-haired girl were lying on a rock forming one body. She'd stopped to look at the sea. She breathed in. At their feet, a scooter and a skateboard. They were kissing passionately. The girl was wearing black trainers, he had on a pair of green Kickers. She could hear them laughing, both of them in the foetal position facing each other, their bodies a perfect fit. It was winter. The boy's leather jacket and T-shirt had ridden up, exposing his lower back and white boxers. The girl was almost entirely hidden behind him. Nora had fit perfectly with the man on the plane. Her nipples were still tender, if she closed her eyes she could almost feel him pinching her. Those emotions weren't for her though, she had long since chosen a tranquil love, the kind she had at home. A forever love. But, rather than soothe her, the foreverness was suffocating her. Why couldn't she be like Robert, who didn't feel the abyss? He was so honest, so solid. Beside the young couple were some headphones and a sandwich wrapped in tinfoil. They hadn't noticed that a seagull had started to peck at the foil.

In two months, she'd need to deliver fourteen illustrations to accompany *The Heart is a Lonely Hunter*, plus the cover work and book flaps. She'd set herself a goal of two per week. *She went into the inside room. With her it was like there were two places—the inside room and the outside room.* She thought about the woman who wrote the novel, she was very young, and yet few writers had been able to create, with such intensity and economy of language, characters so desperate to love and be loved. She was setting up her drawing board, her ten black pencils of different width and hardness. She always sharpened all of them before she started. Then she would feel the tips to check they were the right length, and would prick the palm of her hand with them, leaving little marks. The lead from a pencil always felt cold. It hurt a little. Seeing her hand pricked like that, she imagined a beach where a class of primary school students had been let loose, all of them in blue shorts and green T-shirts, some wearing red baseball caps. The children were the little punctures on her hand. They played football and shouted, happy to be celebrating the end of the school year at the seaside. They were tiny moving dots on the sand that multiplied by the second. She remembered a story her grandfather used to read to her when she was a child, the tale of a mouse with a hundred little mice-children. How many children would she have liked to have? Does anyone really make any of the big decisions in life?

There's a hunched, white-haired man who waits at the entrance to a neighbourhood bookstore. What is he waiting for? He's hoping that one day the woman he loves will enter. He looks scruffy, a bit barmy, and yet, once upon a time, a girl had loved him. That was long ago, but he is still waiting. They told each other the truth and the truth always waits. Peter Pan or Captain Hook? The latter. What the white-haired man with the hunched back doesn't know is that the girl still loves him and thinks him the most handsome man in the world. The truth, always. One day they played with Snowflake the white rabbit, and they painted a processional giant, gave her a pink face. An albino girl had talked incessantly, and a brown-haired boy kept kicking a ball against windows that somehow didn't break. They were happy that morning. One night in Bilbao, they sat at a little bistro table for dinner and the waiter smiled at them, because he'd never seen two customers so in love. They walked down the street and he stopped people and said: she's my girlfriend. The restaurant was packed, couples, a business dinner, even a family with a child, but everything around them was hazy, they loved each other like few had before. At the end of the meal they had an ice fight—the waiter had poured them some shots over crushed ice, on the house. They laughed and hugged, plastered crushed ice over their faces and down their chests; they licked each other and kissed. They wrote each other long letters filled with stories of grandparents who carried cherries in their pockets and women with fishtails for legs. For six years they laughed and made love. They were themselves for six years. Happiness had the contours of their two bodies. In those six years they had what most never attain in a lifetime. I adore you, Captain Hook! Oops—I think we're being watched. Grandmother used to tell her this story when she was little. Nora thought she'd made it up, but now she was beginning to wonder.

Nora had never really made any decisions about her life, and she distrusted those who said they had everything under control. Before getting down to work she liked to have all her supplies ready. She would take a deep breath. Breathing helped her to compartmentalise things. After breakfast, she walked down from the second floor to the ground floor, where her studio was. Both her therapist and her breathing exercises had been with her since adolescence. As had the wall covered with tyre rubber. She'd had one of the walls in her studio lined with rubber from her grandfather's factory. The smell had helped her concentrate since she was a child, since everything had happened. That dark wall. Her grandfather didn't believe in therapy, so Nora didn't see a psychologist, not when her father died (he'd killed himself, but the subject was never mentioned), not when her mother died (her heart gave out, but talking about that was also off limits), not even when her grandmother died (another broken heart). But two years after the last death, when she'd started flirting with an eating disorder, her grandfather found a therapist for her. I hear she's good, the old man said. You should go. She was good, Teresa. She helped her understand. Given your family history, it's a wonder you're not in worse shape, the Buddha-like Senyora kept telling her.

Carson McCullers talks about love, about how only by loving all things can one survive great heartbreak. Mother and Grandmother hadn't known how to do that. McCullers said that writing was her way of earning her soul, of finding God. She did the same with her painting. And now it was Nora's job to illustrate her work, her creation: the mute that survived her. The love of those with broken hearts, or hearts on the verge of breaking, or the love that would heal those broken hearts. While her mind fired off these thoughts, Nora had taken off the smock she usually painted in. She liked working like that, wearing only her white smock and nothing else, it allowed her to be more in touch with what she needed to express. As she removed it she felt something in its pocket. She sighed. I think you're hiding something, a deep malaise, a secret. You, too, are a survivor. You'll have to tell me about it one day, Nacho had said. She thought of Madame Bovary. She'd always found her rather silly, and her conflict, the adulterous love life of a bourgeois woman, ridiculous. Nora walked barefoot on the parquet floor. She kept a bucket of sand from her grandfather's garden and, when she felt her concentration flag, she sank her feet in it for a while. Sometimes, before she started work, she'd sit at the piano and play. The piano was like her breathwork, her rabbit hole, her Alice portal, the doorway into another world. But, for a few days now, she'd felt she was in an altered reality. She wasn't sure where she stood, it was disconcerting. Being in control had been one of her golden rules. She played the first prelude to Bach's 'Well-Tempered Clavier' and thought about the last time she'd played it with such intensity. The day Jana turned ten and her grandfather died. Bach is my God, he used to say; he'll be yours too one day. You and I aren't like them (he was referring to her mother and grandmother), we don't believe in God, it's Bach who rules our lives.

6

THAT AFTERNOON, GRANDFATHER HAD ARRIVED AT THE HOUSE in Tibidabo to celebrate the birthday of his eldest great-granddaughter. It was the thirteenth of June and Jana was exultant. She was like her father, Cloe was more like her. When Nora walked out on to the first-floor terrace she found her grandfather sitting there, looking at the city sprawled out his feet. He was still a commanding presence at seventy-eight, but that afternoon something about him seemed different. Dressed all in white, his hair flowing free, he had the air of a diminished Neptune. She'd always seen him in black, with his hair in a ponytail and wearing a hat. *Avi*, your hair! she said as she hugged him. He kissed her on the forehead, which he'd never done before. He didn't like it: kissing a woman you love on the forehead is for weaklings or imbeciles. Robert, wearing a gold crown that the girls had made, was playing football with them and their friends. Júlia, the close friend and honourary aunt, who never missed a birthday, danced around in a see-through silk dress. Nora and Júlia danced together for a while. They always caressed each other, and Robert liked that, he said they reminded him of two teenagers in love. Nora was wearing a daisy-chain necklace that Cloe had given her, and after bringing out the cake, she announced that it was time for Jana to open her presents: the first one was from Cloe and her.

Everyone went down to the studio, because that was the only place where their present could be delivered. They sang and laughed as they ran down the stairs, and a girl who'd never been there before asked: where are we going? It was a piano concert. Cloe played a couple of simple Mozart pieces (Jana loved Mozart), and also *Sur le Pont d'Avignon* and *El Gegant del Pi*. In between songs Cloe would pretend-fart, and then she sang a darkly comic version of 'Happy Birthday' *a deadly birthday to you, may you have a bad cake, may a tram run you over and we can all have a wake.* Everyone laughed, especially Jana. After Cloe's performance, Grandfather and Jana asked Nora to play something too. She chose her favourite piece, the first Prelude of the *Well-Tempered Clavier*.Robert was still wearing his paper crown and gave his wife a confident smile. He knew Nora didn't like to play in public. When she'd finished, her grandfather told her she hadn't played it well enough. She played it again, six times. That's it, this time you really felt it! And he kissed her, not on the forehead but on her cheek, as he usually did. Nora exhaled. What did her grandfather know about feeling things deeply? Had he ever felt anything deeply? When she was little he used to kiss her on the lips, but then her mother and grandmother told him he shouldn't, and Nora just wanted them to disappear. Sometimes he kissed her when no one was watching and that made Nora happy. She felt special. That important man, who ordered others around and was going to live forever, was kissing her. It would be their secret. Mother and Grandmother didn't understand a thing. And then one day they did disappear. They weren't exactly dead, but they weren't alive either.

'What about Beethoven's *Clair de Lune,* aren't you playing that?' her grandfather asked, knowing full well she didn't like that piece.

'I prefer Debussy's.'

'You should play Beethoven's.'

'Why, Avi? I thought Bach was our God.'

Hearing Nora talk to her grandfather made Robert feel as if he were once again in the presence of the girl he'd fallen in love with. Her tone of voice changed, it became hesitant, higher-pitched. She wasn't aware of it. Her movements were different too: faster, clipped and nervy.

'Bach is our God, my dear, of course he is. But Beethoven's *Clair de Lune* is our life.'

'Did Father play it?'

'It was while listening to his rendition of *Clair de Lune* that your mother fell in love with him. I never told them, but your father's *Clair de Lune* was unrivalled.'

Something about Grandfather was different.

'Why didn't you tell them?'

'Because, I'm an idiot. I've always kept things to myself, unlike your father. Francesc was a great man and a great musician. I, on the other hand, have produced rubber for tyres.'

'I'll learn it, I promise,' Nora said, surprised by her grandfather's words. He'd rarely mentioned his son-in-law before. The subject of the family's dead was taboo. Her grandfather's self-flagellation pained Nora. Hearing him say that he'd taken the wrong path in life hurt worse than if he'd insulted her.

That's how they left it. Everyone clapped and then they all went back up to the terrace to have some cake and open the rest of the presents. They sang. Some of them danced in a circle round the table. It was as if magical beings had taken over the house and its occupants, as if everyone were drunk. Tiny red-faced elves in chef hats, with long ears and golden spoons that served out love, were controlling the party guests like puppets. Robert and Nora danced to a Bulgarian love song that Jana played on the violin. She didn't like the piano, she said she didn't want to play facing a wall. The instrument was a form of punishment, if she had to play with her back to others, then she'd rather not play at all. Nora sat for a moment on her grandfather's lap, the way she did when she was a girl, curled up in a ball. She was happy with the family she'd created, happy in her grandfather's arms. She nestled there and squeezed her eyes shut. She felt like she never wanted to open them again; if it were up to her, she could die that instant in the lap of the old patriarch and life would have been worthwhile. I sense you're hiding something, the man on the plane had said. And how! Her family's history, her own past. Why was it all coming back now? Memories. The week before, Cloe had learned to ride her bicycle without stabilisers. It was the big news of the day. So, around eight o'clock that evening, everyone headed outside to watch her ride her bike. They continued to sing and dance and clap, still in a drug-like haze, led by those green-eared red-faced fairies that marched single file, kitchen spoons in hand. They'd removed their chef hats. Why?

Grandfather had a seizure, he keeled over. The fairies vanished without a trace. Nora, who was walking a few steps ahead with Cloe, turned around when she heard Robert yell. Her grandfather was being held upright in her husband's arms, but his face was askew, half of his body was dead. She ran to him and the old patriarch said: I'm finished. Old as he was, he hugged Nora, with the half of his body that wasn't paralysed, and kissed her on the lips. Jana and her friends let out a collective Yuck! Great-grandfather just kissed Nora on the lips! He kissed her on the lips! His limp body was heavy. Nora shouted for someone to bring the car round. Between the three of them, Nora, Robert and Júlia managed to get him inside and stretch him out on the back seat. He'd wet himself. Nora felt her grandfather's urine on her hands. It wasn't a conscious thought, but there was the sense of an ending. She barked orders. She and Robert would drive him to the hospital and Júlia would stay with the girls. Thank God for Júlia. Words weren't needed. Cloe was saying, 'So we're not going out on the bike then? But you promised!' 'Not right now,' her mother told her, 'you go with Júlia.' 'Of course,' she heard her friend say. During the car ride to the hospital, Nora stroked her grandfather and looked into his eyes. They were open, he was still conscious. In that gaze she could read his entire life. The whole truth was in that gaze. When your hero pees on you, life assumes a different form, and you discover there is an end.

7

THEY ENTERED THE HOSPITAL LIKE IN A MOVIE, RAISING A
ruckus. Grandfather was still conscious gripping Nora's arm.
He was struggling to talk. I'm going now, but don't you worry.
You've been the greatest gift of my life, the best possible
granddaughter. We adored you, all of us, especially your
parents. They weren't weak, they loved each other. I just
couldn't see it, but your grandmother did and that's why she
went with them. It's taken me my whole life to understand.
You're not like me, Nora. You're not like them either. You're
better. Forgive me for everything I didn't do. Forgive me and
remember: we're all blind ... Nora put her finger to her
grandfather's lips but he continued ... building a museum
for those who are not yet here ... I know, Grandfather, now
rest. I've loved you too, more than I've loved anyone. There's
nothing to forgive. She kissed him. He added only: be yourself! Then everything went really fast. They whisked him
away, an hour passed and the nurses wouldn't allow them to
see him. Nora demanded to be with him: he was her grandfather and she didn't want him to be alone in a cold hospital

room. She insisted she wanted to hold his hand. It worried Robert to see his wife so agitated. He held her and tried to comfort her, but she only wanted to be by her grandfather's side. She rocked back and forth in her husband's arms, her face flushed, as he tried to stay calm. Bastards! Can't they see it's the end? The nurses said they were following protocol, they couldn't ignore the rules, but they tried to put her at ease; they, too, had had grandparents, and they would let her in as soon as possible. Finally, a nurse opened the door for her. Transitioning is rarely without some indignity. There he was, struggling to breathe. It had been years since she'd seen his naked body. The end is always difficult, and more so for those who have been strong. It reveals all our false myths. His body was now just a bag of bones and loose skin. She noticed a spot on his chest, a blemish over his heart the size of three tennis balls, some of it raw skin, some of it covered with scabs. How long had he had it? Why had he never mentioned it?

She thought of tennis balls. Her grandfather had been good at tennis, and Nora had started playing with him every Wednesday evening, because all his old tennis partners had died. He still wanted to play but had no one to play with. So, he teamed up with his granddaughter, who really wasn't good enough, though she tried. Why hadn't she seen the spot during one of their games? He must have known it was there. He'd been hiding it for years. Even those we love most are a mystery to us. She should have suspected something when he told her months ago that he didn't want to play anymore, that he wasn't in the mood for tennis. Death begins when desire ceases.

Nora told him to move his right arm; he swung his left arm. Not your left arm, your right! He swung his left arm with even greater force; he couldn't stand not being able to carry out an order. How am I doing? If you find me a job, I'll do it well, I won't let you down, I promise. That was when Nora realised the kind of man her grandfather was, a man who'd built an empire from scratch. He was exactly that, someone who, entrusted with a job, gave it his all, never let others down, and always made those who had taken a chance on him shine. He never stopped being that boy from humble beginnings. He was always a clever, hardworking man who made others look good; no one ever regretted taking a chance on him. For the first time she understood that her grandfather had never been as powerful as she'd believed. She massaged his feet and legs and looked at his frail body. He was no longer speaking, but every now and then he moved his left arm and Nora would remember his *I won't let you down* and would stroke him and say: Avi, you're doing great! You've always made me shine. The doctor said he'd had a stroke, they would have to move him to a bigger hospital to know the extent of the damage and for follow-up care. When Nora asked about the spot on his chest the doctor told her it was skin cancer. Was he being treated for it? I don't think so, Nora said. The doctor repeated the bit about the stroke, the other hospital, said he'd receive better care there. He'll be properly monitored, you'll see. Doctors are a different breed.

In the ambulance, she kissed her unconscious grandfather and remembered his kisses. That was what growing up really meant, she thought, losing your loved ones. All the things that are important to us slowly vanish and cannot be replaced. During the ambulance ride she would have liked to ask him about certain things, but she knew it was too late. Who had her father been, what kind of man was he? Why had her mother's heart imploded? And he, who had he loved? Had he ever been in love? Who had her grandmother been, deep down? But, Nora said nothing. How can you talk to someone who isn't there anymore? What can you say, when the one who would have replied is already in the throes of death? *Adéu*, goodbye. It wasn't just her grandfather she had to bid farewell to, but everything she had been when she was with him. There would be no one from her childhood at Christmas dinner. She noticed that one of her tears had fallen on his cheek, the man who'd meant everything to her, but she wasn't crying. She hadn't wept when her father died, or her mother, or her grandmother. Maybe she would begin now. The wailing of the ambulance seemed to amplify her pain. There was a spare tyre on the floor of the ambulance, near her grandfather's feet. She touched it. She breathed in. She stabbed the palm of her hand with a pencil from her handbag, drawing blood. Often, physical pain could make her forget her mental anguish. Her hand was bleeding but she hardly noticed. She'd punctured her hand but couldn't feel the pain. The ambulance drivers were listening to a cookery programme: *and now we'll season the apples and place them … .* Her grandfather had loved to cook. The doors of the ambulance opened and someone spoke to her; she was still hugging him. At the hospital, the doctor said it was the end. Nora didn't need anyone to tell her that. It had been a bad stroke and, at his age, he wasn't expected to last more than three or four hours. Grandfather held on for forty-two. They removed his dentures to prevent him from swallowing them; dying with no teeth was not something he would have liked. She and Robert took turns so there would always be someone holding his hand. He died at seven p.m. on June 15th. The girls didn't see him again. She preferred to leave them with the image of him at the party.

Nora thought again about the night they'd spent together. They'd had their own private world. From the very beginning, from the day she was born, they'd formed a different kind of family. One where she and her grandfather belonged to each other. They struggled to understand other people. Grandfather, who had played at being God, was really the most vulnerable of mortals. Nora felt disoriented, as if she didn't know where she was. From that moment on she'd carry with her a piece of tyre. She shut herself away to practise Beethoven's *Clair de Lune* and played it at the funeral mass. I won't let you down, Avi. The expressions that our grandparents favoured leave their marks on us. Maybe her father had killed himself because he believed he would never measure up, that he would always let them down.

When she'd finished playing, the four-hundred people clapped. Some said that she'd played like her father. She looks so much like him! Poor man, what a waste, he would have been so proud ... . Nora was perfect, wasn't she? Why were they talking about her father now? It was her grandfather they should be talking about. She had no clear image of her father; after his death, the photographs of him had disappeared. Clapping is not usualsual at funerals, nor is it frequent to see so many people at one for an eighty-five year old man. I won't let you down. She was him. She needed the smell of tyres. Throughout the mass, and later when people approached the family to pay their respects, Nora rubbed a freckle on her right arm. She was holding his hand when he died. She'd felt him slipping away a few hours before, and had asked the nurse to sedate him. His hand squeezed hers and then went limp. He was there one moment and gone the next. Now she really was alone in the world, nothing stood between her and death. Are you sure you're not running late? that White Rabbit of a London taxi driver would have exclaimed. Nora felt like Captain Ahab pursuing Moby Dick. She closed his eyes, kissed him on the lips, and whispered the prayer her mother used to recite when she was a little girl: Now I climb into bed, with seven angels I rest, three at my feet, four at my head ... Grandfather had hated the Church and anything associated with it. But it was the ritual that mattered, repeating those same words, which were among the few her mother had uttered after her father's suicide. Why was she remembering this now? She hadn't thought about any of this for years, she'd practically wiped it from her memory, to rid herself of the pain. The last kiss she'd given her dead grandfather had felt like other kisses. She was lost, willing to do anything. I see what is, and what is not.

8

NORA WAS ONLY TWO YEARS OLD WHEN HER FATHER DIED, but she had a memory of that day. It's your fault he's dead! Her friends, as well as Teresa, her therapist, said it was impossible for her to have memories from that age. But, she knew that's what her mother had screamed at her grandfather when her father killed himself. After that she barely spoke again, but when Nora was five, her mother told her that her father had killed himself (taken his own life, she had said) because he felt he couldn't live up to Grandfather. Nora's father was a concert pianist and teacher. Her mother fell in love with him because his fingers played her like they did the piano, his eyes too. Nonsense! her grandfather always used to say. Nonsense was also his response to her mother's accusation that day. The issue was never broached again. Mother never screamed again, never opened her mouth again, except to utter a few odd words, and she never laughed again. It was almost as if she didn't even breathe for all those years. But Nora did. She didn't miss her father, she hadn't known him. She felt disgust. How could he kill himself when his daughter was so little? Why? Her mother didn't speak, she only said that nightly prayer and kissed Nora four times. Nora waited for that moment; first her grandfather would tuck her in, when he was home of course, then her mother would say the prayer. It was the only moment in the day when she heard her mother's voice, when her mother looked at her, for her gaze was always fixed on the horizon of the walls and she didn't budge from the piano bench that had belonged to Nora's father. She spent her days on that bench, as if she were glued to it. With slow, circular strokes her fingertips caressed the red velvet, and with tight lips she hummed the same melody.

Grandmother combed Nora's mother's hair, she dressed and fed her ... but not Nora. She learned to do everything for herself. When school was out she'd spend the day with her grandfather, and he taught her about the business. She whiled away the hours sitting in his office. A table was built for her, and placed beside the captain's own enormous desk. Captain, that's what they called him. She drew at that table, and Grandfather hung the drawings he most liked on the walls. Nora worked hard so that her artwork would be displayed. She drew and breathed in the smell of plastic, the whole building was redolent of tyre rubber. Grandfather was alive. She could concentrate on what she liked most. Whatever you do, do it well. It was her grandfather who'd started taking her to museums. When they got home, her mother would be staring blankly at the piano bench, and Grandmother would be combing her hair. She liked

Grandfather better. One afternoon they got home, as they did every day, and her mother was dead. Nora didn't cry. She missed the night-time prayer, but she no longer had to see her mother tethered to that bench, staring at the wall. A living death. Her heart gave out, she died of a broken heart, Grandmother said. It finally happened, thought Nora, who was only seven at the time. That's ridiculous! Grandfather had exclaimed. I've heard it can happen, a rare condition, affecting 0.1 per cent of people (her grandparents spoke in percentages), a broken heart resulting in heart failure. Our daughter's heart broke the day Francesc died, Grandmother said. Fine. I'll see to it that my granddaughter's heart never does, I'll see to it that she takes after me instead of her weak parents, who aren't around anymore. They've both abandoned her! Grandfather had yelled. That was what Nora had always believed: her parents were weaklings who had abandoned her. Only strong people remained by her side. Only strong people loved her. But now her grandfather had said just the opposite. Her parents hadn't been weak? What about her? Should she be counted among the strong or the weak? Who was she, and what side was she on?

Then it was Grandmother who moved to the piano bench. Grandmother could have joined the land of the strong, but she chose the weak. Cari, the woman who helped to care for her mother, now looked after her grandmother. Nora and her grandfather were still out in the world, living. During the day, Grandfather was at work and she was at school, and they spent their afternoons at the company, among the tyres.

She drew while she listened to her grandfather making decisions, running the business. And Grandmother stared at the wall that would forever guard their secrets. Sometimes Grandfather would disappear in the evenings. Nora never knew where he was. Grandmother cried. Her heart gave out too. It happens.

Nora continued playing the piano; she had to draw the mute in McCullers' novel, but her fingers couldn't stop. Maybe the weaklings weren't so weak, nor the strong as powerful as they appeared. Maybe it really was all your fault! She glanced angrily at the framed photograph of her grandfather on the piano. White hair, smiling eyes, black T-shirt against the blue background. Nothing more. A newly-recognised fact surprised her: that complete strangers, or seemingly trivial situations, can change our lives. Sometimes a stranger can be the punctuation mark that alters our sentences. She thought of him, the way he'd touched her. She didn't want to think about him, but she did. His face, the smile that was also reflected in his eyes, his way of looking at her. His Catalan, which was inflected with his native Segovian accent. I'll always struggle with Catalan, I'll never be truly bilingual, he'd said. Nora slipped on her robe, rubbed her earrings with fidgety circular strokes, and again noticed something in its right pocket. She pulled her hair up into a bun and studied her reflection. She couldn't remember the last time she'd looked at herself in a mirror. She thought it was silly: we are what we are, why the need to look? But now, wearing those earrings she felt the need, she felt transformed. She opened the robe, revealing her breasts, her thighs, her flat belly. She looked at herself, naked in front of the mirror, with her hair up and those earrings on. Who did that body belong to? She'd never identified with her own body. But now, the way she saw herself held the beauty of a work of art.

It was his card in the pocket of her robe, that's what she'd felt; she didn't want to admit it but she'd spent the whole morning touching it. It was an elegant business card. Nacho Santillán, Marine Biologist. A telephone number. She hadn't wanted to look at it, just feel it; she did it unconsciously, as if behind her own back. She stroked the edges of the laid paper with her fingertips and cut herself, then licked the blood off her index finger. But she didn't remove it from her pocket. Why? That would mean acknowledging his existence, and the fact that she wanted him. She knew what was on the card because that morning she'd transferred it from her travel bag to the pocket of her robe and sneaked a glimpse. She should have tossed it into the fireplace. She fantasised about consigning the card to the flames. It's what it deserved, to burn. But she couldn't do it. Fire was something else that took pride of place among the things Nora liked, a much shorter list than the list of things she loathed. She wasn't capable of making any decision regarding the card. She chose an enormous canvas and started to paint. That wasn't what she was supposed to do! She painted in the same way she'd played the piano all morning. From the splotches of paint emerged the naked body of a woman and a blindfolded man wearing trousers, a black sports jacket and a hat. The woman was wearing the Countess of Segovia earrings. Her legs were spread, her arms extended from her sides, and her hands rested against a window. Her back was turned to the viewer, the only thing visible was her hair, which fell past her waist to her buttocks, and her profile, a nose that looked much like her own. Who was this man? Out of the corner of her eye Nora spied her drawing board with McCullers' book and her black pencils on top. She thought of the children on the beach. She needed to work. Why didn't she? She touched her earrings, her lips. She was strong. This world is for the brave, the old man used to say. To phone or not to phone. Grandfather's final words were: be yourself! She felt guilty because instead of doing the sketches, she was working on a strange painting and playing the same pieces on the piano. The naked bodies on the canvas, who were they? Who was that woman with her legs spread? Casual love is reasonable enough, but is it love? She removed the card and dialled the number. Since their time on the plane, she'd belonged to him.

She was shaking, she felt pressure between her legs and in her chest. I, too, am weak! *Hola. You've reached Nacho Santillán's voicemail, please leave a message.* At the sound of his voice she started to sweat, she was breathing heavily. She couldn't believe what she was doing. She was faithful, a faithful wife. Days can be long when you're falling for some-one; you don't want to phone, and he doesn't call. Days can be never-ending. She didn't say anything, she just took off her robe and played *Clair de Lune* again. She felt the cold jangle of the earring against the phone. It hurt a bit. She sensed the piano bench's velvety warmth beneath her sex.

When she finished playing she said: 'Bach is our God, but *Clair de Lune* is our life.' Why had no one noticed she was dead? Why had no one taken the time to bury her? I am not. And if I am not, I am dead.

9

SHE OPENED THE REFRIGERATOR AND ATE HALF A MANGO, savouring it, giving herself time. Then two tomatoes and a glass of white wine, just the right amount of alcohol to counter the excitement she felt. She didn't need any more for lunch. While she chewed, she stared at her mobile. Now what? Would he call? No one had ever broken her heart and no one was going to break it now. Like her grandfather, she was a survivor. Nacho had called himself a survivor too, he'd said he knew they were both hiding a secret. Survivor of what? She went back to her studio, sat at her drawing board, and attempted a charcoal sketch of McCullers' character. Everyone in the novel believed they had found in Mister Singer, the mute, the only person who could understand them. Nora tapped her teeth with the end of the pencil, twirled it around, and resumed her tapping. The sentence she'd heard some days earlier in London resounded in her head: My name is Paul Smith Page, but of the two surnames only one is real. What if the taxi driver was the character from the novel and he'd mysteriously recovered his voice?

What if his words had triggered what had happened later? What was he trying to tell her? Everything had changed after that sentence. People who bite their pencils are insecure. By contrast, tapping one's teeth indicates concentration, will-power, determination. Grandfather's maxims, which she repeated to herself. Ever since her flight, she couldn't get that white headrest with the blue lettering out of her mind. During both of her pregnancies she'd dreamed of water. Why had no one noticed she was dead? She didn't want to live without someone who would pinch her nipples.

Her phone rang. Her face creased into an expression of victory. He's hooked too, I knew it! I'm not hooked on him though, I'm only doing it so ... then the look on her face became subdued. It was her husband, saying he'd be home early. Cloe was having a sleepover at a friend's, and they could have a romantic dinner. What would she do now if Nacho called? Robert, I might have to meet my publisher. Your publisher? At dinnertime? Yes, go figure, he's asked me, you know what they're like ... but it's not confirmed yet. I'll tell him I can't. I'd love a dinner date, let's see if I can make it work. I love you. Great, see you later. The *I love you* had been hers, his had been the *see you later*. It had been more than a year since her husband had suggested a romantic dinner. Better this way. She'd have supper with her husband and forget the rest. That guy wasn't phoning her back or showing any signs of life! She should make a decision and be done with it. But, she couldn't. She was confused. When you're torn like that it's best to let life decide for you. Her green eyes were expressionless. She needed to breathe, empty her mind. She hurled her mobile at the sofa. He's not calling. Arsehole. It had been a long time since she'd played the seduction game and she was out of practice. She'd forgotten the frustration that precedes and follows desire, if she'd ever even felt it. She was beginning to think she wasn't cut out for such games, she should just carry on with her life as it was.

The red sofa was a six-seater they'd bought in Paris. Robert had been smitten by it. She'd had it shipped to Barcelona as an anniversary gift, but it had never looked good anywhere in the house. It had ended up in her studio. Nora wasn't complaining, she liked it, it was like falling asleep wrapped in the curtains of a classic theatre; she'd had some of the best siestas of her life on that sofa. Her mobile was lost in an expanse of red, it looked like a tiny critter abandoned without water on a desert dune. Nora stole a glance at the device. She continued to struggle with the sketch of the mute. She rendered him plump, with sausage-like ankles, his too-short trousers hanging low on his hips, his clothes too small for him. Then she tapped her teeth with the pencil and rubbed-out part of the sketch ... to hell with him! She slammed the pencil on her desk; it bounced off and fell on the floor. Naked on the red sofa, she covered herself with a Persian wool blanket. She eyed her phone and slid it under a cushion. Pathetic. The pencil was under the desk, now with a broken tip. She'd have to sharpen it. What would her grandfather say if he could see her now? Nora was lying in the foetal position facing the wall; she felt the blanket on her body, her fingertips traced circles on one of the red cushions, while her other hand fingered the earring that was pressing against the sofa. Goal: to forget about her phone. She closed her eyes and felt his hands, his tongue on her face. He had a wide tongue.

The room was palled in darkness when the landline rang. She was dreaming that she was at her beach apartment on the waterfront, and a campervan with a neon sign that read RAINBOW had appeared on the promenade. In the dream it was also night, but on the terrace next to hers a woman was energetically cleaning the railings and wiping some golden balls with a cloth. She looked a bit like Mary Poppins, and she carried on shining those balls with a product used to polish metals. Her white cloth was turning black. The beach was deserted, save for the tractor cleaning the sand and its driver Joana, a friend of Nora's. She waved to Nora and traced the outline of a fish in the sand. *Be yourself!* Joana called to her. The neighbour continued to polish the globes. Nora was intrigued, she felt the need to touch them but she didn't dare. A great bolt of light suddenly emerged from the globes, stretching all the way to the campervan's neon sign. RAINBOW. The Mary Poppins next door, in a pink headscarf and a red-and-white plaid robe that came down to her knees, began to glide across the ray of light. It had become a great bridge, linking their terraces to the campervan. *Are you coming?* her neighbour asked, extending her hand. Nora took it. She was wearing a low-cut, flowery nightdress that had belonged to her mother. They walked barefoot across the lambent light, and as they approached the van, she noticed that one of its walls had been painted with a jungle scene, in the middle of which stood Pocahontas and a giant fish that had leapt from the water and been immortalised in midair. It wasn't the best place for a fish. Though it was the middle of the night and a wind was blowing off the sea, Nora wasn't cold: a special kind of warmth radiated up from the luminous bridge and through her bare feet, enveloping her whole body. She saw, before she could answer the landline, that it was her husband calling.

'Nora, what's up? How's it looking? Are we on for dinner?' While he bombarded her with questions, she fumbled under the cushions for her mobile to see if he'd phoned.

'It's looking ... good! Yes! We can have dinner.'

No sign of Nacho. She didn't want her frustration to show.

'Nora, is everything all right? So, you're not seeing your publisher then?'

'I told him I couldn't make it.'

'Great! I'll be there in a little bit. I'll pick up some sushi.'

'There's no need.'

'I think we should.'

'Whatever you want ... Robert, are there any golden balls on the terrace railing at the beach apartment?'

'Sorry?'

'I thought that the railing on the terrace had gold balls on it ... Never mind, forget it. I'll be waiting for you. I'll lay the table with some candles.'

She had the best of husbands; what was she looking for in the man on the plane? What if it had been a dream, a spell cast by the taxi driver, but then, what about the card, the earrings ... could she have made all of it up?

She switched on the lamp over the sofa and saw it was eight o'clock in the evening. Still no call! Of course, she hadn't left her name. What if her message hadn't been recorded? What if his call logs weren't showing? What if something had happened to him? What if the other night, after dropping her off, he'd had an accident on his way to Sant Pol? She'd never know. She couldn't stand the thought of never seeing him again. In his world, she didn't exist: if something happened to him no one would notify her. Everything they had shared reverberated in her mind, in that space between brain and eyes, as if trapped in a never-ending loop. The touch of his hand, how she yearned for it. To not have him, not be with him, was too much pain. Losing Nacho would be like turning to dust, but she wouldn't be empty inside, her feelings for him would remain, they were something she'd never experienced with anyone else. Perhaps only that night with Grandfather. Had she fallen in love? How did her family figure into all of this, where did this leave them? Robert was one thing, but what about the girls? Having a family did not lend itself to fooling around and going nuts. Grandmother had succumbed as well.

10

NOT A VERY PRODUCTIVE DAY WHEN IT CAME TO WORK: HALF a sketch of McCullers' mute. She hated herself when this happened. From her spot on the sofa she eyed the morning's painting. Drawing distanced her from what felt most real, it forced concretion on her. She needed a change. Freedom. Who were those people, those two figures? You have Robert to protect you from the outside world, especially from other men, Júlia always reminded her. Why wasn't that idiot saying anything? She was filled with dread at the thought that he might be dead somewhere along the Maresme coast, and no one would know to tell her. The two of them didn't exist as an entity. She had to talk to Júlia, tell her everything, but she wasn't ready to verbalise things yet. She googled Segovia; it reminded her of some of her favourite towns in the Baix Empordà, only larger and without the sea. She wanted to go and live with him in a small Segovian palazzo, at the home of the countess who had died for love. Love vows that have never been made cannot be broken. When the person one loves commits suicide, where does that love go?

It solidifies, becoming a stone in the body of the person that is left, until one day that person turns to stone and dies from rock-hard solidity. Sadness is like a stone, once inside a person, it kills. Love hardens too, and dies from grief. No one should live a sad existence if it can be avoided.

She left her mobile in the bedroom because she was disgusted with herself, checking the screen every five minutes. She hoped Bach would help her forget things and find her way back to her husband. The story with the man on the plane made her feel like a fool. *E se domani*, the Mina song, announced the arrival of Robert, sushi and white wine. They had made love for the first time to that record. She climbed the stairs slowly, wearing the countess's earrings, her hair in a top bun, held in place with a sketching pencil. Robert turned to look at her as she walked into the living room. By way of hello, Nora removed the pencil. On the table, sushi, wasabi, fresh ginger, wine already poured. They sat down. He'd taken off his tie. Feel like playing a little? Sure, Nora said. He blindfolded her. He fed her, gave her sips of wine. With every bite, he touched her and she let herself be touched. How are you doing, Nora? He kissed her neck. I'm fine, why? Another kiss. No, nothing. We haven't played around like this for a long time, and he gave her ear a little nibble. I miss it too. Play with me, now the other ear. I want to be your whore.

She knelt over him on the floor, and every time Robert moved to kiss her she pulled back. She knew it aroused him, having his desire frustrated, alternating between submission and control. They played the game of cat and mouse for a while, until Nora let go and went slack as a doll. Robert laid her on the table and stood at one end of it. She was blindfolded and imagined it was Nacho. When he entered her she couldn't hold back, she sat up, tight against her husband's chest, and they came together. He carried her up to the bedroom in his arms. He left her on the bed and went to the bathroom. Nora checked her phone for messages. There were none. It was eleven o'clock. Robert came back to bed; lying on their backs looking at the ceiling and holding hands, they burst out laughing. We're getting better at this every day! What was it you said earlier about some gold balls? Oh, nothing, they're on the railing at the beach flat. Are you sure there are gold balls there?

They continued to laugh. We need to do this more often! I'd almost forgotten how good it could be. Then, like every night, her husband fell asleep; a few minutes later he was snoring. Nora wondered what Nacho was doing. You can't substitute one love for another, the same is true of desire. Robert's hands were big and strong; she caressed them from wrist to fingertips and remembered what they'd looked like twenty-five years earlier. The reddish hairs on their backs were white now, the freckles were turning into spots. Having a lover improves one's marriage, now she understood what that meant. Her mobile pinged. The screen lit up her night stand. She wondered for a few moments whether to look or turn her phone off. The message was an address in Pedralbes, a house. Nora slid closer to her husband and kissed him; he stirred and uttered a few unintelligible words, then rolled over. Like a log. The sleeping pills. He had his back to her. Nora slipped on a little black dress over her thong and finished getting dressed, then put on her coat. She tiptoed down the stairs holding her stilettos in her hand. When her green Mini Cooper pulled out of the garage, she knew where she was headed, but not what she'd find there, or in what state she'd return. It was a cold night in late February, most of the bars and cafés had their shutters down. The streets were deserted. A winter silence, deeper than in summer. Where was she going? Somewhere, to be with him. Why?

The quietude of the snow unnerved her: it seemed to halt everything, only the beating of her heart continued. Both in the snow, and when she swam underwater, she always felt as if she were floating, as if she were immortal. She didn't want to die, the world continues after death, and the dead leave it all behind. She thought of her parents, of what life would be like if they were still alive. The silence of riding a bicycle along the seafront on a winter's morning is not as deep as the silence of the snow. She wanted to live. She drove on, heading towards the Pedralbes district, towards the unknown. She didn't recognise herself or her actions. There was still time to return to her husband's arms and listen to him snoring. She held the tension of the wait in every one of her muscles, the fear of facing the moment that filled her with yearning. She drove and thought of the gold balls in her dream, how shiny the woman had left them. She wanted to hold them. She thought of lemons and oranges. Her grand-father had told her that if they didn't touch then they wouldn't go mouldy for months. The key was for them not to touch. When Grandfather explained that to her she'd thought about the solitude of lemons. Maybe they wouldn't grow mouldy, but if in order to last they couldn't go near their own kind then it hardly seemed worthwhile. What was she up to? Was that what *The Blue Angel* was about, the film she and Robert liked so much? The fall from an upright, moral citadel of rectitude into a pit of one's own making. What was she doing? Living, letting go, going with the flow. The worst part was that her husband was a good man. Her daughters, they no longer needed her. She pictured the breasts of that Mary Poppins neighbour of hers who polished the gold balls. She wanted to be with him.

11

THE TRAFFIC LIGHTS WERE ALL GREEN. SHE PRESSED THE buzzer at the address she'd been given; a wooden door swung open, following the command of a metallic female voice. It was one in the morning and there was no one on the street. The only sound was the municipal cleaning crew, going around with their water hoses, cleaning up what people had dirtied during the day. A gravel path led to the house, the main façade of which was covered with bougainvillaea. A door opened by itself. There was no one there. She slipped off her dress and put her coat back on over her bodice. A path of candles led her to a room from which a light emerged. She enjoyed the sense of instability and pleasure that her high heels evoked. Nacho was waiting for her in a round bathtub, which was il-luminated from beneath. *Clair de Lune*. More candles. Nora let her coat drop to the floor. They didn't speak. She could feel her heart beating. His eyes x-rayed her. Have you ever been in love? No reply. Nacho interpreted her silence as one that required no answer. He got out of the tub and wrapped himself in a black terrycloth robe that was draped over a standing hanger, a clothes rack of worn wood with several legs that reminded her of a makeshift scarecrow. It made Nora think of Dorothy saving the scarecrow who longed for a brain. Her grandfather had read her *The Wizard of Oz*. She never could decide which was worse: not having a heart or a brain or courage. *The road to the Emerald City is paved with yellow bricks*. I like what I see, bumpy head. Put on your coat and come with me. He took her hand, pressed a button that opened a door, and led her onto a terrace overlooking the city. In the centre of it stood a waterbed surrounded by patio heaters. The waterbed was covered with a thick duvet. It looked like a magazine ad of a place you might dream of living in but where no one actually lives, and at the same time it evoked a strange feeling of unease, of sadness. A cardboard world. He removed her coat, let his robe drop, and pulled her towards him. They looked at the stars. She was wearing only her pearl thong. They breathed out. Other than taking her hand and caressing it, he hadn't touched her yet.

'Have you ever been in love?' he asked again.

'I'm not sure.'

Her parents had been in love, and it hadn't done them much good. But, had she ever been in love? She'd been with Robert for twenty-five years. Before him there had been only one other boy, in her teens; she'd promised never to tell anyone about him, and she never had. Nacho's fingertips traced circles on the palm of her hand. Robert shielded her from the world, from other men. She loved him. But, was that the same as being in love? They held hands and looked at the night sky. She thought about the friends she used to stargaze with. Max, who was no longer there, and Joana, who lived on a beach and cleaned the sand with her tractor. Nora and Max used to chase ants with their fingers. She realised she was no longer breathing fast. She was there, with that stranger, and she felt at ease. He wasn't doing anything to her, just holding her hand, and every now and then stroking her palm with a fingertip.

'Think where you'd like to be touched and I'll do it,' Nacho said.

'Sorry?'

'Go on.'

She felt the need for him to caress her belly. Nacho caressed it. She wanted him to lick her ears, she didn't want him to touch them, she wanted him to lick them, inside and out, and tug on her countess's earrings. She was still fantasising about this when she realised it was no longer only happening in her mind.

'Do you want to have a go?'

'I won't know what to do.'

If you think you can't, you can't. If you're sure you can, then you can, her grandfather used to say. Nora was looking at Nacho. He'd closed his eyes and was waiting for her to touch him. But where? She kept looking at him, wanting to get it right, but he was giving her no clues. She went for the lips, started kissing him. He pushed her back.

'Wrong!'

'What do you mean?'

'You did what *you* were in the mood for, not me.'

'How am I supposed to know what ...'

'By listening to me. You're a painter, right? So when you paint, where does that come from?'

So, now she was supposed to explain to him how she went about making art? When he was still in nappies she'd already lost her father, her mother, and her grandmother. She took a deep breath. She had this. She lay down beside him without looking at him. She gave herself time, listened to her own breathing, felt the night air, the warm bed. She crawled under the blanket and began to lick his big toe, first the right foot, then the left, then both, he made no effort to resist, she could hear his controlled moaning. She stopped and pulled his hair, and he pulled hers. It hurt. They looked at each other as they pulled each other's hair. When she slapped him he didn't slap her back. Nora spat in his face and then he rubbed it against hers. She had no idea where any of this was coming from. They pulled each other's hair again, and suddenly he slapped her bottom. She liked it. Now you need to yield. He lay her down. He massaged her with lavender oil. Nora couldn't remember the last time her husband had given her a massage. The *Clair de Lune* had begun to play. Her grandfather's tricks working their magic again. She thought she glimpsed a princess carriage flying high above the terrace. She awoke from that dream as he was entering her. He was fully inside her, she'd never wanted anything so much, and yet she'd begun to weep. I can't! He withdrew. Nora rolled over on her back and curled up, facing away from him. He massaged her neck. He was there, present, while she carried on crying. I've never been with another man.

No one had ever touched her like that before. The only thing she disliked was his absence. As he caressed her he said only:

you're good. Just then she wished he would suck her breasts, and he did, tenderly, gently, first one then the other. He upped the pace, bit her nipples. It was starting to hurt. He continued with the biting. She straddled him. That's when he slapped her. They pulled each other's hair and she rode him. She let herself be guided by what she was feeling. She was no professional, no pervert, she was just a regular wife who'd always been faithful, who loved her husband and had just had sex with another man. She felt pleasure she'd never known before. She started crying again. I've fallen in love with you, she told him. He had just branded a mature woman the way you brand cattle. Nacho thought of his mother's bluish face and the man who vanished in the dark. Then death. She hugged him fiercely and he reciprocated the intensity. They lay like that for a while. Before she could fall asleep, he took her in his arms, covered her with one of the blankets, and carried her to the round hot tub. She noticed that the walls in the room were all mirrors. Naked in the tub together they saw themselves multiplied many times over. It was cold and she was tired. She had no idea what time it was. How long had they been together? She could still feel him inside her. Inebriated by his presence, she saw, in the mirrors, his image repeated infinitely.

'Do you have to go?'

He seemed to be reading her mind.

'Yes.'

'How long since a man bathed you?'

'I don't know.'

She twirled around in the tub, her arms at her sides, and every now and then he caressed her, smiling at her playfulness.

'I can tell you like mirrors.'

'Not at all.'

'It doesn't seem that way. Come here, you're cold.' He wet her with the shower head—warm water, good pressure—starting at her head and then slowly moving down. 'Spread your legs more.' He covered her eyes with a silk scarf and put earplugs in her ears. He kissed her. Nora was overcome with the fear of abandonment. He tied something around her waist, some kind of chain that felt cold on her skin and slid down her hips. She felt it over her buttocks and pelvis.

Who was this man and why had he chosen her? Was that what people meant when they talked about passion? He ran a sponge with rosewater soap over her body. He kissed her lips, and she felt his member rubbing against her from behind. She wanted him to enter her again, but he didn't. He continued to wash her, rinsing her with hot water. She liked it at a temperature most people would find too hot. He removed her earplugs. Fear of abandonment, a terrible panic at the thought of not having him. If he were to vanish she might die of grief. She couldn't afford that, there had been enough broken hearts in her family. She peeked out of the bottom of her blindfold and glimpsed the silver chain around her hips.

'You take hot water well,' he said. 'I know what you want, all you have to do is feel it and I know. We won't do it again, you need to get home. You wouldn't want to be found out just as we're starting , would you?'

She kissed him and tried to guide him inside her, but he shook his head gently and lifted her out of the tub. Then she heard. More! I want more! Again, you whore! It was coming from the next room.

'What was that?' she asked, untying her scarf.

'A mirror of sound reflecting what we've just done. In this house, the walls retain every moan of pleasure and give it back as an echo.'

'I heard a couple fucking.'

'You heard correctly. It's just friends I share the house with, but I live in Sant Pol, as you know.'

Nora was silent after that. A couple doing it in the next room? They could've seen her! She couldn't go around having sex with people so close by. She'd counted seven doors on the way to the terrace, so it was only logical for him to share the house. But it was after five in the morning. Had those friends also been screwing all night? There was a whole world out there, so much going on! You need to get out more, Júlia always told her.

'Don't worry, they're very discreet, and besides all of us press a button before we leave ...' Nora didn't follow the bit about the buttons. 'Those earrings look good on you, the silver chain too. I have another present for you.'

'I don't want any more presents. I want to know when I'll see you again.'

'Hey, what's with that tone? What's the rush?'

She had to leave. She'd go home, climb into bed, hug Robert and pretend none of it had happened.

'I'm leaving.'

'That's it? I don't get a kiss?'

'Don't play with me, Nacho. You know I wouldn't leave just like that ...'

'I know. Will you accept my present then?'

'Yes.'

'Close your eyes and wait.'

She heard him leave the room and return presently. He opened her coat, pulled down her bodice, and pressed something onto each nipple. She wanted him to pinch them again, but he didn't. Don't peek, wait until you're alone at home to look. You'll like it. Something to remember me by. He rearranged her bodice, buttoned up her coat, and kissed her on the lips. His restraint undid her, his power over her. Her subjugation.

'I've fallen for you too', he said, and just then the moaning started up again in the next room.

'Your friends are very active', she said.

His words weren't lost on her.

Leaving the house, walking away from that hot tub, from him, filled her with a pain that was almost physical. Had she? Been in love? She could feel whatever it was on her breasts. She felt her nipples. She wouldn't look until she was back in her studio. What would Robert be doing? She switched on her mobile. There was a message from Júlia, nothing from Robert. How goes it, queen of the night? Nora didn't reply. They'd talk tomorrow. She needed the time in the car for herself. She'd just had sex with a stranger and was on her way back home and into her husband's arms. And tomorrow? Would she tell Robert that she loved him? What would that mean now? Of course she wasn't the first adulteress in history; she had friends who'd kept lovers for years. But Nora had always believed it wasn't for her; that if she ever found herself in that situation, she'd be honest about what was going on. But what did it mean to be honest? She drove along and again realised she loved Robert. She felt she loved him once more, with a feeling less encumbered by boredom since all of this had started. Robert appeared to her more as the man he'd been in the beginning: free, attractive, with his own life and interests. She loved Robert and the girls, who were no longer girls, really, and who'd said to her, Mamà, but you only left yesterday! They no longer needed her as they once had. What was happening to her? She felt like the sea: it's windy during the day, the waves lash, then evening falls and the water is still.

As all of this ran through Nora's mind, Nacho was giving himself a water massage in the hot tub. Then he fell asleep. When he awoke to the groans from the next room he had tears in his eyes. Music boxes that stopped playing, how he hated that! When he was a boy, his mother or father or siblings would always wind his music box before it stopped playing; after his mother died he hurled the box from the aqueduct into an imaginary sea. When he swam underwater he imagined himself being pierced in the heart by a spear gun. Another recurring image was that he was being violently dragged by a fishing hook that was caught on his cheek and half of his face was ripped away. He had chosen not to tell Nora about it. He was afraid of falling in love, afraid of loving and losing again. He hadn't loved anyone after his mother. But he'd break free from the fishing line, he would not end up in the hands of the fisherman, the man who had been with his mother that morning. He would not die by that criminal's hands. The king of pain is stronger than any evil. He thought about the woman he'd just spent the night with: they were so different they might be mistaken for the same person. We'll come to our end, you and I, just as the dinosaurs did. We'll leave no offspring. Only a few bones for the archaeologists.

12

ROBERT, LYING FACE DOWN ACROSS THE BED, WAS STILL snoring. He looked peaceful. Nora felt the need to hug him and tell him she loved him. She had just crossed the threshold into an unsettling world, a wayward universe where *I love you* always means something else. What were her feelings for Nacho? I love you—who should those words be for? Love shouldn't be exclusive. The key was to determine the ideal distance between two people. She and Nacho were founding a new world, building a kingdom without being fully aware of it, one vast enough to encompass everything, yet so small it could hold only the two of them, so beautiful it was invisible to everyone else, as indestructible as the mightiest among them, the strongest man and woman in the world, the two survivors: themselves. Nacho wasn't intimidated by her. Nora had noticed that, with the exception of Grandfather and Robert, men were afraid of her. But Nacho sat and smoked at the mouth of the cave while others slept their lives away.

She went down to the kitchen to make herself some herbal tea. While the water boiled she studied the long strip of blue fabric that hung by the window. She'd taken it from her grandparents' house. She saw herself as a little girl, looking at it as she was now. It was a massive shopping list with everything you could find at the market—Grandmother always called the market 'la plaça', the square. In the middle was a large yellow spoon and a green fork of the same size, and beneath them stood three tiny cooks with red faces and hands, wearing white chef's hats and smocks, yellow boots with green shoelaces. Their eyes were two black circles, their mouths just an outline, their noses a downward facing crescent moon. It seemed to her that those tiny beings came to life. They were forest elves who protected the house from evil. It hadn't worked for her grandparents, but it had for her, and her daughters had grown up with them. She remembered all those mornings in the kitchen, with Cloe talking to those little red elves. What are you doing? I love them! Passionate and oblivious to her surroundings in equal measure. Sometimes her daughter reminded her so much of herself it was almost painful. There were six elves altogether. The three on the bottom, one that dangled from the tip of the fork, and two others resting on the fork and the spoon, their mouths not a circular outline, but a crescent moon in the same shape as their noses, only bigger. Back in her bedroom, she slipped on an old T-shirt and snuggled up to her husband. He gave off warmth like a heater. She fell asleep.

'You didn't hear the alarm?'

She looked at him without replying, barely able to open her eyes. Robert was tying his tie. There was a time when he'd said he'd never wear one. He kissed her on the lips. That was new.

'What time is it?' she asked.

'Ten o'clock, we overslept. You look tired. Are you all right?'

'I had a hard time falling asleep. You were snoring.'

'I'm so sorry. It must be the sleeping pills.' Another kiss on the lips. 'Try to get a little more sleep?'

'I can't! My sketches beckon ...'

She told him she loved him. Her eyes closed. She made an effort to open them again and Robert was gone. Her gaze lingered on the painting he'd given her, the face of a black-eyed woman with a small mouth, the sensual kind of nose that puffs up or flattens depending on what she's feeling, red hair wrapped in a gold scarf, and a blue dot in the middle of her forehead. Growing up without parents makes you see life differently, Nora thought; there's no one before you, no ascendant link: you are the only one. She woke to a slamming door and Jana's loud voice downstairs. She'd been dreaming that she was on a vast empty beach. It was night. In the middle of the beach, there was a white campervan with three purple lines across the bottom, and a large neon sign spelling out RAINBOW on the roof. Nothing else. A sea with no boats, a beach with no town or city, no birds or people or dogs or seagulls. Only the sea. The white sandy beach. The camper-van. Nora seemed to have been dropped from a helicopter; she walked along naked, her breasts sagged, she was ageing. She was drawn to the RAINBOW because light issued from the van. It looked like God's envoy to Earth or a spaceship from the 1960s. What was inside? Why was there nothing outside? Where were the houses, the people? She opened a window in the back of the vehicle and saw her: the ballerina from 'The Steadfast Tin Soldier', spinning on a round pink platform. She was wearing the countess' earrings, her right foot en pointe, left leg folded over her right leg, arms in the air. Nora slammed the window shut. She hated music boxes and classical ballerinas. Horrid! Alone in the world, naked, with the ballerina. The idea of drowning herself in the sea was starting to appeal to her. The van looked familiar, recognisable. She was growing old. The music had changed, now 'Che Farò Senza Euridice?' was playing. This time, instead of opening the window she opened a small door, she could only fit through it on her knees. The ballerina had disappeared and now a gypsy woman was belly dancing. She signalled for Nora to come closer. She too was wearing Nora's earrings. I like you! she called out. Her hips gyrated sensually, a large orb was drawn on her forehead. She noticed Nora's silver chain. Sexy, she said. I want one. Here, you can have it. No, this one is yours.

'Mamà, are you okay?'

Her daughter was standing there, tall as always, next to the bed.

'Jana. I missed you, too many days without seeing you. How's everything?'

Nora looked her over slowly, from head to toe. She'd turned out so tall, her girl, and pretty.

'I'm good. And you?'

'What are you doing here?'

'This is my house, too.'

'Of course! But you're gone so much ...'

'Mamà! I study, I work, I have a boyfriend.'

'I know, darling, and I'm glad.'

Her girl had grown up. What would she think of Nora's recent activities? Better for her not to find out. Jana had always had strong, uncompromising opinions. Like Grandfather, and Robert, that phrase they all repeated about doing what needs to be done.

'It's noon, Mamà. Why are you still in bed?'

'Rough night. I had trouble sleeping and couldn't shut out your father's snoring.'

'Lluc snores as well.'

'Really? You must leave him! Darling, mark my words: don't get involved with a man who already snores at twenty-three.'

Jana was so much like Robert; her aplomb and resolve, her desire to act professionally and be of service to others. From Nora, she'd only got her eyes.

'Your father didn't snore at that age.'

'What are you talking about, Mamà?'

'Never mind. Listen, Jana, do you happen to remember whether there are any gold balls on the terrace railing at the beach?'

'Now I know you're mad.'

Jana hugged Nora and kissed her twice.

'Call me if you need me, okay?' she said. 'I just stopped by to get some clothes. Lluc and I are moving in together!'

'Oh, that's fantastic. I so want you ...'

But Jana was already gone.

'I so want you to be happy, at least a little, and to never have to live a lie.'

As soon as she'd spoken, she thought those last words were daft. Lluc and Jana were moving in together ... .

She recalled a morning fifteen years ago as if it were yesterday. Robert was away on business and she was taking care of everything and looking after the girls; at night she would collapse into bed. That morning, toward the end of the school year, Jana woke her up already dressed and holding her still-ringing Mickey Mouse alarm clock in her hand. What's the matter, Jana? It's eleven in the morning, Nora. It was that phase when Jana called her Nora. But Jana, it's not even six o'clock! Don't make any noise or you'll wake Cloe. It's eleven in the morning, Nora, my alarm clock says so! She was pointing to the round yellow-eared thing, with Mickey Mouse drawn on the face of the clock, his hands marking the time, his left the hours, his right the minutes. Jana was looking at her with a huge grin on her face, so proud that she'd got herself dressed and been the one to wake her mother. All grown up. She stood there the way she had today, the same eyes, the same look of innocence. How could Nora be putting the happiness of her loved ones on the line? And for what? She'd managed to persuade Jana to turn off the alarm clock and climb into bed with her, and they'd slept until eight. That morning, before the school run, Jana told her she wanted a skeleton for her birthday. A really big one, okay? With everything, bones, heart, lungs, a bum. And she'd got her skeleton. They still had it, down in Nora's studio. Jana II. She'd named it herself. She was going to be a doctor.

13

SHE FELT THE SAME EMPTINESS SHE'D EXPERIENCED WHEN they left Jana at summer camp for the first time. Thirteen nights and fourteen days, no phone calls allowed. Jana was six years old. And the same devotion. Waving goodbye to that bus filled with boys and girls, her daughter's smiling face pressed against the window. She hardly ever asked anything of God, but she'd prayed that all would go well. Jana's best friend, Maria, sat next to her, looking like an abandoned puppy; if she'd been told to get off the bus she'd have jumped at the chance. But Nora's daughter was leaving happily. It was a rite of passage. You put your child's happiness before your own fears and tribulations. Why don't we do the same for our partners? Now Jana was off to live with her boyfriend. Just like that, no warning. Did Robert know? How would she ever explain to her daughters that she had a secret life? And how would these two young women handle the truth? What was the truth? That the man she'd fantasised about and desired since the London flight wasn't her husband, but someone else entirely? When she took off her

T-shirt to put on her work smock, she saw her nipples: two black hearts the size of prunes. She was suffused by a sudden, intense warmth. Her life shouldn't be governed by the impact that her actions might have on two young women, even if they were her daughters. Her task, now, was to determine the locus of her existence. What about her own mother? Nora barely even knew her, not in her undamaged state. What would she have thought of what was happening to her now? Having donned her smock, she headed downstairs to make herself some coffee. Jana was moving in with Lluc. Nora rubbed her smock over the silver chain on her lower belly. She was transformed, queen of a distant land, a woman, and she felt her femininity as she never had before. Since the flight, through Nacho, the void in her life had closed, the abyss was gone, or at least there was the fantasy of its disappearance, a fantasy of instant happiness.

Sitting at the kitchen table with her fourth cup of coffee, Nora took another turn with the red-faced minichefs in their white toques. She'd put on her countess earrings. She checked her phone. Nothing important. A message from Robert saying he was leaving for Brussels, something work-related, he'd be back in four days, and hugs and kisses. Nora went down to her studio, ready to face not only the mute but the entire world of McCullers' creation. She wouldn't waste time today. Before getting started, she took off her smock and looked in the mirror. The way she saw herself held the beauty of a work of art. She thought about the house in Pedralbes and what had happened there. The moans she heard, which Nacho said were from the couple he shared the house with. The way they did it, the way he washed her, and his question: have you ever been in love? She chose another canvas, very large, two metres by two metres and forty centimetres. She was painting again. A female body, a silver chain. McCullers' ten drafting pencils lay undisturbed on the table, but she couldn't peel herself away from the canvas. She'd told Robert she loved him. She was doing nudes with acrylic paint. Two women and two men, their legs and arms intertwined.

She looked up at the sky. She would have liked to live among the clouds, materialising and dissolving every day. A parallel could be drawn between the evolution of art history and the arc of natural light throughout the day, going from the clearly demarcated and schematic Romanesque all the way to William Turner, pure atmosphere, texture, colour. Piero della Francesca would be a chiaroscuro, the blend of dark and light. A voyage from a simple world to an increasingly sophisticated, dramatic one. I see what is not there, she'd told her grandfather when she was very young. What was she up to now? Still in a painting frenzy. She kept at it for five hours, then collapsed on the sofa. She realised that the life she'd known until then was drawing to a close. She liked watching the sky from her studio, from anywhere really. The sky and the sea. She felt trapped if she couldn't see them, like the woman playing the harp in the yellow Bjørn Wiinblad poster, bought years ago in Copenhagen, which hung at the foot of the bed. She'd fallen asleep with that image ever since. A round-faced woman with tiny feet standing on tiptoes, trapped inside a harp. The woman is flying, it's the harp that is playing her. That was Nora's life.

We often don't realise that our taxi driver or the server who just brought us our coffee has a life of their own. Nora walked over to the rubber-lined wall of her studio, sank her face into it and inhaled. The feeling of missing herself when she was with Robert, missing the person she was and missing Robert too, had been with her for too long. She had an idea for a new painting: a naked couple, moments after making love, he's kissing her and her face is blue. That English taxi driver called Paul Smith Page, he was also flesh and blood and one day he would die. He had triggered a new life for her. There were so many ways to die, what would his death be like? Poor McCullers, who would paint her mute? Are you sure you're not running late? the taxi driver would have asked her if he'd been the White Rabbit. She painted because she couldn't accept reality as it was. She saw what was not there but should be. The best had already happened. Nothing would be better than the present moment, and before now there was nothing. There is only one story in life. The moon reminded Nora that she'd been brave, she'd followed her desire. The previous night, driving on the ring road around Barcelona, the moon had had his face; there had been fewer people on the streets, fewer cars. Silence reigned over the city. She had no regrets.

14

WHEN NORA ILLUSTRATED A WORK SHE FELT AS THOUGH SHE was shedding light on it. She'd read *Heart of Darkness*, about Kurtz's quest to bring a civilising light into the shadows of the jungle. But Kurtz had succumbed to his own darkness, the darkness in his heart. She too was falling to pieces. It was six in the evening and she'd made no headway with that lonely, hunting heart. Every time she sat down to start work her feet led her to the canvas. Only two things interested her, that man, and painting nudes. I see what is there and what is missing. She was working on the painting of the blue-faced woman who looked like her; the man kissing her was Nacho. They were there, they had just made love, and perhaps moments later they would no longer be part of this world. The painting had captured that instant. The silver chain seemed to glow from within. But a short respite alone is safe; in time, cares become modified, and the absent love decays and a new one makes its entrance. She stared blankly at her wall of quotations, this last one from *The Art of Love*. Her mobile rang.

'I'm in a playful mood. Want to play?'

How thrilling to hear his voice!

'Play what?'

'The game, no questions.'

Here was someone versed in the art of love.

'If you want to play you have to accept the rules, no protesting, no responding.'

He spoke in the same deep voice, with the same aplomb.

'I'll decide what you do and what you don't do.'

'When will I see you?' she said without listening.

'I said no questions.'

'Nacho, what are you on about?'

When he hung up, it hurt. She hadn't been able to hold her tongue.

'I want to play!'

He'd answered the phone; she could hear his slow breathing. His silence spoke louder than his words.

'I promise not to ask any questions.'

'All right then, let's play. And because I can see you understand and accept the rules, I'll let you in on a secret I've never shared with anyone. I was born dead.'

Silence.

'"... My father had given me up for dead and was on his way out of the room when I revived. It was my mother's faith, her love, that brought me back to life. She believed in me without even knowing it, simply by opening her heart as much as she could.'

Nora didn't say anything. She pictured him lying dead on his mother's breast, her eyes fixed on him, concentrating with all her might on resurrecting him. Then the infant breathed, smiled; newborns don't smile, but he did. His just-born body wriggled closer to suckle his mother's nipple. Lost in these thoughts, Nora scarcely noticed that Nacho had continued to speak, and then he hung up. She was alone again. He had said something to the effect of: a friend will pick you up shortly, do everything he says; you won't see him again.

Every time he hung up Nora felt an emptiness. But now she couldn't phone him back. She was part of the game. She had to wait for this friend of his, even though she didn't want to see him, it was Nacho she wanted to see. She was starting to think that the taxi driver's words had unleashed an alternate reality, a world where she was no longer herself, one controlled by seagulls. Maybe Nora had also been born dead and someone had slipped inside her body in that impasse between death and returning to life, and now she was possessed by this other person. Why should she comply with Nacho's demands? And now she'd agreed to his game and could pose no questions. She slipped on a rose-blush silk dress, a garter belt and black boots, and used a perfume that always put her in the mood. She sat in the living room on the first floor, her eyes on a drawing Cloe had made when she was four: that's me. The man would be there any minute. Her daughter's self-portrait was all straight lines and circles. Cloe had been at the age when children draw everything like that. The ears, two circles; the hair a bunch of straight lines down to her waist. Nora could still see in her daughter the child she'd been, the same expression. What would Cloe become? She said she wanted to be a physicist. Yes, I'm going to specialise in quantum physics, and one day I'll prove to you that magician-chefs exist in another reality.

The doorbell rang. Nora took a deep breath. She put on her coat and hat. It was cold outside. She set the alarm and left the garden light on for when she returned. An old and solid-looking gold Mercedes was waiting for her outside. She knew nothing about cars, but this one seemed hideous and very long. The chill reminded her of the snow that in recent years had visited the city every winter. She wanted to listen to the silence of the snow. The last time it had snowed, the entire city had come to a standstill and, in her car, she'd cruised through the silence of the neighbourhoods from the seafront up to Tibidabo. The twenty-minute journey had taken three long hours. It wasn't snowing today, not yet. A bad feeling came over her. It seemed to her that she wasn't going any-where specific. A seagull had stopped at her feet and stared at her with dead eyes. They have orange beaks and feet, white heads, necks, and bellies; their backs are grey, their tails black. They waddle along the shore and peck at the sand. She thought of Nacho. They were so different that one day, someone, somewhere might even mistake one of them for the other. Why was she playing along?

15

EVEN BEFORE OPENING THE CAR DOOR SHE SAW THAT THE driver was a man of about sixty, smartly dressed. He was still attractive. Grey hair, beard and moustache. He was looking at her out of the corner of his eye. Ready? Yes, Nora replied, not really knowing what that meant or why she was saying it. The man drove silently while she told herself that no one really chooses anything in life. She didn't dare look at him or even turn her head in his direction. She fixed her eyes straight ahead and occasionally turned toward the side window, which she'd rolled down. She wanted to smell tyre rubber but didn't want the man to notice. It was as if her grandfather was still there, lurking within her, still alive. She'd felt trapped these past years with Robert and the girls, but now, with this thing she'd embarked on, she wasn't free either. Her black beret made her feel protected, as if the man in the driver's seat couldn't possibly know what she was thinking.

She recalled Grandfather's theory of women and vases. He'd told Nora about it when she asked him why he hadn't remarried. Grandmother had been dead for five years. I've had my vases, he said. You're grown now so I can be frank with you. I was never faithful, Nora. I started seeing other women soon after marrying your grandmother. It was all a game. I did it out of lust, out of need, to blow off steam after work, but never to find another vase. It didn't conflict with my values because I loved your grandmother, the others were just a distraction; like going to the movies or playing tennis or doing crosswords. Your grandmother was my vase, the finest vase in the world. The rest of the women, well, they were all second-rate. Let me tell you something about vases. When you've taken three good looks at one, it loses its appeal, except your own of course. I never went with another woman more than three times. I inspected the vase this way, that way, and by the third time I'd grown tired of it. There aren't that many good vases on the market. As soon as I sensed that one of those women wanted to become my vase, I would vanish. I already had my vase.

Nora was seventeen years old when her grandfather told her this over dessert one day. On the one hand she couldn't suppress a smile, thinking what a brute her grandfather was and how feminists would have had a field day with him. On the other hand, she valued the fact that he'd been honest with her and was clear about his priorities. At that moment, Nora had exclaimed: but your vase has been broken for five years! Your vase doesn't exist anymore! My vase is still the same, there will only ever be one vase in my life, and its flowers: you, your mother, your daughters ... there's no other vase or flower for me. I can look at them, admire them at times, but I don't want them. Keeping a vase is no easy feat, and I've had enough complications, too many. Having a close relationship with a woman brings pain. I prefer to be alone now. Nora choked up when she thought that she would never have another conversation with her grandfather. There were few people as frank as he was. Something small and dark flitted past the window, a bird maybe. The birds were her grandfather, she thought. Every morning a great tit visited her terrace.

She observed the hand on the gear stick, a bony hand, the kind she liked, with a wedding ring. Maybe the man was a silent messenger who would usher her into Nacho's arms. We all create fantasies in order to live, Nacho had told her the other night. She needed hers, she realised, but she wasn't so sure that being in the car with this man fulfilled any of them. Would he be there, wherever they were headed? Just as they were setting off she had heard the stifled cries of a seagull and had been filled with a sense of foreboding. She had only got in the car because it linked her to him, and now, riding down a side street in Poblenou, she couldn't shake the presentiment. She noticed a boy with a yellow balloon tied to his wrist; she imagined the knot in the string coming undone and the balloon floating away, the boy weeping, the balloon vanishing in the infinity of the sky. She wanted to be that yellow balloon.

They pulled into a warehouse full of martial arts equipment. They were surrounded by piles of tatami mats.

'This is what I do. I distribute these to gyms and health clubs around the country', the man explained. His deep voice reminded her of Leonard Cohen.

They were standing in a sea of tatami mats.

'What am I doing here?' Nora asked.

'No need to act naive,' the man said. 'Take off your clothes.'

Nora turned her back to the man and started to undress, feeling very insecure. For a few short, almost imperceptible moments she was filled with doubt, but she did what the man told her, she unbuttoned her coat and placed her beret on a tatami mat. What kind of game was this? Why was she undressing instead of telling the man that this was all a mistake? That what she wanted was to be with Nacho, that she only did this kind of thing for him? What was the man doing while she disrobed? She didn't want to look, she felt vulnerable, she didn't know why she was acting the way she was, but for some reason she was going along with it. After the coat, she unbuttoned her blazer, her eyes on the tatami in front of her. They were good quality tatami bases, made of mahogany, and futons of different widths. She wondered which of those tatamis they would do it on. She was in a daze, and barely managed to react.

'Every now and then I'm in the mood for sex,' the man said. 'Sex with a woman other than my wife, I should say. Like today. I take a shower, I put on some nice clothes, my best cologne, and I do it. No, don't turn around. I want to watch you undress without you seeing me. You're the best-looking woman I will have fucked.'

Nora didn't know whether to run or cry. She removed her stockings.

'Good. Now put your boots back on.'

She complied with his request. The man continued.

'It relaxes me for a few days. I hope you enjoy it, too. I'm going to cover your face with a blue cloth. The only woman I have ever loved died a long time ago while we were having sex. Her face turned blue. She wasn't my wife, so I ran. I was scared. I abandoned her. She was married to another man, but she was mine more than she was anyone else's. I've never been able to be with a woman whose face wasn't covered with a blue cloth. You remind me of her. You're prettier, but your skin has the same liquid coolness. When we're done, I'll lay you on a tatami mat, kiss your blue lips, and leave. A taxi will collect you and take you home. You'll never see me again. These tatamis are unrivalled, there is nothing better when it comes to resting one's body and soul. You'll see.'

Nora let her panties drop to the floor and felt him take her by the neck, though not hard enough to choke her, and with his knees he parted her legs. The blue woman in her painting. But why? She felt the stranger's enormous cock from behind. Nora imagined it was Nacho. The man's hand grabbed her breasts and, discovering the black heart pasties on her nipples, began to caress them: I see you've come prepared, you were told. I like it. Seconds later he ripped them off, both at the same time. That's when he came.

Then everything happened as he'd said it would. Very gently, he laid her on the tatami mat in front of them and covered her with a thick blanket. As he kissed her, a tear soaked through the blue cloth onto her cheek. I always search for you, he whispered before disappearing. She could still feel the warmth of his body, and the burning sensation on her nipples.

If you are floating on your back in the sea when a plane flies by, the image you are left with is of Jesus on the cross, being propelled through the air by two streams of smoke that merge into one. Christ courses horizontally at great speed, driven by those two lines of white gas. This Christ goes forth, always onward, and for a short while, the time the flight takes to complete its journey, the mortals in its hold feel like birds. They smile, filled with fantasies of a sought-after destination. If, for some reason, the Christ plummets, everyone weeps. It was winter, but Nora imagined she was floating on her back in the sea. Swimming in the sea in winter gives you a different perspective on life. Why was she painting things that ended up happening? Nora didn't believe in God but she did believe in the sun. She was searching for Nacho. Where was he? She was already dressed when her taxi arrived. The man in the Mercedes was right: that tatami mat did rest one's body and soul.

16

FOR TWO DAYS SHE SCRUBBED HERSELF RAW WITH A YELLOW glove, trying to wash away what had happened. What was Nacho playing at? And, what about her? He was still MIA. In the bathroom there was a photograph of Jana at the beach, lying on the sand where the waves broke. Nora sat wrapped in her white terry robe, her gaze lingering on that summer morning many years ago. Watch it roll me over, Mamà! Look, look! A wave came, shifted her a few centimetres, and to her it was the most important thing in the world. When we are children we dwell on what's important, then we forget what that is. Whenever Jana felt frustrated, Nora would sit her down in front of that photograph and say to her: remember that moment, because that's life, a little wave that rolls you over. But that wasn't cutting it now. I need you to fuck me, she'd just texted him. Radio silence. She needed a reply but it wasn't coming. She knew she was jonesing for him, she'd allowed herself to be weak. Few things in life were more infuriating than having a crush on someone who reciprocates your feelings and then disappears.

The power of absence: hours go by and the obsession only grows, and there comes a point when you'd do anything to be with that person. She thought she'd moved beyond this. She felt primitive—like an animal.

Júlia said she had to learn to control herself. You can't tell him I need you to fuck me! Why not? Because *he* has to say it. So, now her ultra-liberated friend was conventional? And Nora hadn't even told her about Tatami Man. Nora had never understood the rules of flirtation: men have to play one part, women another, and if the roles are reversed then it doesn't work. Nora did what her feelings told her to do in the moment. That's why she'd been attracted to Robert: her husband didn't expect a woman to be sensual and alluring while laying the table, simply because she was a woman. I need his touch. For two days that was all her mind parroted. The mere thought of Nacho filled her with a powerful, warm sensation. She hadn't heard from him in forty-nine hours. She needed to work. She would have liked to enact her own *Themroc*, the movie where Michel Piccoli turns into an urban caveman; she'd lock herself away with Nacho in that house in Pedralbes, board up the door, and feed on the flesh of passersby. No talking, only communicating by guttural sounds. To return to primitiveness. She remembered seeing the movie at the Cinematheque with Júlia and Max when they were fourteen. Piccoli's character turned his bedroom into a cave. Max said he was going to do the same; years later he killed himself. The slow disappearance of those she could call with her heart in her hand, to talk about anything, made Nora aware of the passage of time. She felt like an undertaker. Max was one of the few people she had known who could listen without judging. She would have told him what was happening to her and he wouldn't have told her that she couldn't say I need you to fuck me. He'd taken his own life with the shotgun his father used for hunting rabbits. The guttural sounds in that movie had led her back to her dog, Aton. She realised he sounded like *Themroc*. Her mastiff didn't commit suicide, he'd died of old age, like Grandfather. The strong don't kill themselves, they succumb to old age, but the end result is the same. Nora was more and more alone. The death of loved ones admits no substitutes. Those who are left behind, who live on, grow lonelier by the day.

She opened the box that held her collection of turtles. Grandfather had given her little turtles as presents. That strong man couldn't take the death of any more loved ones, so he would give her only toy turtles, nothing alive. She lined them up and looked at them for a while as she sat on the cold floor. She particularly liked the silver one with the head that opened up, with a little silver spoon inside, a miniature sugar bowl. She'd phoned Nacho nine times that day: he wasn't answering his mobile or offering any explanation about their game. To please him, she'd done it with an old geezer. Why? She thought he'd resurface after that, but instead, nada. What was the point? Why did he want to share her with others? And why had she let him? A work of art is always the fruit of the artist's imagination, and she'd begun a series of paintings of bodies in the act of love. She recalled the day that Joana phoned her in tears because her pet turtle had committed suicide by plunging from the sixth floor. Júlia was going to kill her. How can you stoop so low! His refusal to answer her calls, the sheer disrespect, filled her with rage and fuelled her yearning. The pressure between her legs didn't let up. Nacho had told her he wanted her, caressed her like no one had before, and then vanished. She hadn't remained faithful for twenty five years only to have to rein herself in now that she'd broken her vows. What had this game been about? Robert's work commitments were taking longer than expected, he wouldn't be back until Sunday. It had been a couple of days since the girls had set foot in the house. Nora wasn't worried about Jana, but Cloe? She'd phone her later to check on her.

She thought about the man in the Mercedes and the life he led, how he'd said that sometimes he craved sex with women other than his wife, and when he did it, he found release. He'd talked about the dead woman and the blue scarf. She'd painted the scene without knowing the story. Tatami Man reminded her of the yellow ceramic turtle her grandparents had brought her from Cyprus, he stretched his neck in the same way. Then he calmed down. Are you sure you're not running late? A rabbit grin from ear to ear and that oversized pocket watch. Taxi driver by trade. Guardian of a new kingdom. She was still looking at her turtles and had started returning them to their box when the phone rang. It was her publisher. He was apologising. The McCullers project is a no-go, Nora. I'm so sorry. I feel terrible. They've cut our budget, the publishing house is really struggling right now. I'll try to make it up to you, and of course you'll be paid for the work you've already done. All she could say was, I understand. She liked how the publisher pronounced her name, he had trouble with his r's. She wondered whether he felt the same as Tatami Man, the need to be with a woman other than his wife.

She would finally have the freedom to paint whatever came to her, without any guilt. A new exhibition was in the offing. She liked the periods in her life when she was preparing for an exhibition, they were like pregnancies. She wasn't fully present and yet she felt rooted, connected to the earth. That morning she hadn't worked, but she had repotted a ficus, a pothos and two magnolias. Before transferring the plants she'd buried her feet in the soil of the new pot, and for a few moments it eased the anxiety of waiting for him to call. She had trouble admitting the anguish caused by the absence of a man she'd only known for two weeks, and the fact that a complete stranger can suddenly change our lives. How our lives can turn out one way, or be entirely different. How I love you always means something else. These thoughts obsessed her. That was what her paintings were about: the unbearable banality of it all ... and addiction. We all arrive at our knowledge of love by having loved a few people, a few faces. Who could love and hold in her mind every face at once? A whore. A love whore. She stood in front of the mirror again. She held the yellow turtle from Cyprus against her belly. She pulled her robe open and ran the cold turtle up and down her body. She was wearing her countess earrings. I didn't want to draw that mute anyway. She left the turtle on the red sofa. Nacho was still missing in action. She needed him to touch her. She dangled the silver chain over her sex. And her own husband, he was away more and more.

Liberated from sketching, she tackled another big canvas, even larger than the one she'd done a few days before. She painted a woman standing up, naked, behind her an older man was wrapping her head in a blue scarf. Yet again! I can only do it with women who have a blue scarf over their heads, the man in the painting was saying. He looked like Turtle Man. If they don't have a scarf, I can't get it up. The last time I had sex with the only woman I've ever loved, she turned blue and died. Painting those figures brought her pleasure. She'd also felt pleasure in the warehouse, though she didn't want to admit it. New places often seem hostile. It was plain that the woman in the painting had found herself naked in a new place, strewn with tatami mats, but whatever misgivings she'd had disappeared when the old man behind her started caressing her. Such dismal progress with her mute, and then these paintings just flowed out. Nora walked over to the canvas and rubbed her nipples on the blue paint. Like the woman in the painting, she'd wrapped her head in a blue silk scarf, this one from the trunk that held her daughters' costumes. She lay on the red sofa and caressed herself with the yellow turtle; she fantasised that she was standing naked outside her front door, with a smartly dressed Nacho, who made her lie on the ground and tapped her with a cane.

Sharp little taps, but gentle at the same time. Her finger drew circles with the paint that was left on her nipples. She had just orgasmed. The turtle was between her legs. I see what is there and what is not there. She needed to touch him. She sent him another message. Reply or you will never hear from me again. His message arrived in less than thirty seconds: Barcelona Princess, by the Forum. Room 330, 4 p.m. Wear a domino mask and the silver chain. I'm sending a car. Maybe now she was discovering what the distance between them should be. She had forty minutes.

17

THE LATEST DREAM HAD TAKEN HER BACK TO THE BEACH, BUT now a giant fist had crushed the RAINBOW campervan. Where its four walls had stood, a boxing ring had been set up on the sand. Nora pulled up her black stockings. She chose black again, this time an open-back dress. Wearing stockings turned her on, the feel of them against her skin. Two brawny young men were in the ring practising full-contact kickboxing, surrounded by a crowd of naked people. A little silver bell rang and they started fighting. Sometimes it was two young men with tanned, oiled skin, other times their faces had been replaced by hers and Nacho's. They boxed with their Greek-god bodies and glistening skin, and all the naked spectators shouted their names. They queued to watch them fight. While Nora put on her stilettos with black velvet trim and the mask she and Robert had bought in Venice, she thought that, at the moment, Nacho was clearly the winner. She did everything he wanted. But boxing matches are unpredictable, and in kickboxing one is allowed to use one's feet. She had always been obsessed with keeping the right distance in her relationships with others. So, why am I still wearing this silver chain? Why am I doing this? From the bathroom window she spotted a white limousine with blacked-out windows coming to a halt by the front door.

She had no way of knowing who the driver was. As she emerged from the house the rear door opened on its own. She climbed in. She couldn't see the driver, tinted glass separated them. The car started moving. She thought of Cloe. She still hadn't heard from her daughter and hadn't even tried to contact her. She WhatsApped her. Will you be home for supper? As she messaged she fantasised that the man behind the wheel was Nacho; they'd stop somewhere and make love right there in the car. But the car didn't stop. Nora saw her masked reflection in the mirror that covered the floor of the limo. She could see her feet from below. She understood why some men had foot fetishes. She didn't know what to think, her fears were returning. What was she doing dressed like this, in a car that was taking her to the Barcelona Princess Hotel, sending a message to her daughter? It was ridiculous, a woman her age! What was awaiting her? She tried to picture the scene. Erotic foreplay with handcuffs, blindfolds, a mouth gag. She was starting to realise that she was into that kind of thing. She had just sniffed her little piece of rubber. She was doing it for Nacho, she felt he was watching her. Maybe this time he'd be there. If not, then what?

A photo-shoot setup awaited her in room 330, around a red carpet, and a spotty boy who could easily have been Cloe's age. He seemed impatient. The room was circular. The only thing there was the camera setup. The two of them were surrounded by black curtains. A man could be hiding behind those curtains, Nora thought. She was squeamish about young men, sexually speaking, the idea of doing it with someone her daughters' age was repulsive. That boy had never thought about being shot with an underwater gun, nor about being fish-hooked through the mouth. But he did mention that he'd paid good money for her. And Nora finally understood. It wasn't a game. She felt a stabbing pain in her stomach and chest, something between asphyxia and the urge to scream. Her reaction was swift and calm, as if she'd been doing this her entire life. She complied with her customer's requests. That's what the boy was. Nacho was a pimp who was selling her body for a pretty penny. Nora was a high-class hooker. She could have left, of course, but she didn't. She wanted to punish herself. Deep pain imparts profound lessons, she'd learned that as a child. What doesn't kill you makes you stronger. Nietzsche, from her wall of quotations. She was paying the price for her foolishness. It was just business.

How could she have fallen for the stranger on the plane? How could she have thought it was love? Had they really built a world that belonged to them alone? Were they different enough to be mistaken for each other? She was beginning to understand. She wept silently as the spotty adolescent thrust his member inside her. She couldn't stop thinking what a good actor Nacho was. She'd fallen in love with him, but what about Nacho? Even if he'd been using her from the get-go she couldn't entirely rule out that he'd fallen for her too. While she was ruminating on these things, she'd quit her body and forgotten all about the young man. She could feel him inside her again; he'd grabbed her breasts. Nora didn't say anything. She felt dirty. Are you crying? The boy caressed her cheeks as if petting a dog. Sorry, gotta go. You've been fantastic. Cheers!

She was doing all this—why? There she was, lying on a mat having just been fucked by a boy who could have been her son, and felt utterly repulsed. The man she loved only wanted her as a whore. She'd fallen for a pig who was profiting from her body. To make matters worse, she was discovering that she actually enjoyed sex with strangers, and that despite the mess she was in, she wasn't completely turned off. Feeling pain gave her pleasure. The boy was a nobody, a sorry messenger. It was Nacho who'd caused the pain. But, even though she felt that hurt deep inside her, somewhere no one else had ever reached, she still wanted him and wondered when she would see him again.

She didn't want anyone to see her crying; most especially, she told herself, Nacho would never see her cry again. She wanted to rip off her earrings, but she didn't. The worst part was that when she thought of him that warmth spread through her body. Despite it all she kept asking herself when they would be together again. We all have our private lives, but do you realise we're also part of something bigger? I sense you're hiding something, a deep pain, a big secret.

You don't have to tell me if you don't want to. I have the feeling that you're a survivor, too. Indeed I am! He had no idea to what extent she was a survivor. Yes, she was afraid of death, she knew first-hand all that departed would be missing. But she was even more afraid that life would deal her a bad hand. What she felt now was pain, and she was an expert at avoiding pain, she dodged it by working hard and willing herself to carry on. If she could push through when she lost both her parents and her grandmother, how could she not now? A mere change of scenery does nothing if the problem resides within you. Have you ever been in love? Yes, you bastard. With you. She thought about Robert too. She was beginning to understand that their love was the familial kind. Her husband had been a self-preservation strategy, a protective shield that had prevented her from seeing the hidden pain that resides in all things.

Her sealed lips formed a straight line. She was beside herself with rage. Her phone pinged. Sí, Mamà, I'll be home for supper and to spend the night. Can you make a potato omelette? Nora wept silently, covering her face with her hands. She didn't want anyone to see her like this. She didn't want to see herself. She shook with each sob, but made no sound. It had always been hard for her to cry. She'd been struck and she was sinking, but she had no intention of abandoning ship. It wasn't her style. The image of seagulls gaining ground in the city and gobbling up children's sandwiches filled her with sadness. She'd hit rock bottom. Now she would start to rise, passing others who were on their way down. She imagined herself as a lemon, Robert as another lemon. If they didn't touch each other they could still last a long time. Nacho wanted to play. So, let the game begin. She thought that watering plants was a form of prayer.

18

NORA MADE THE POTATO OMELETTE, HER BODY PERFORMING the required movements, her hands all the steps a good omelette entailed. But her mind was on the seagulls and watering the plants. A plucked seagull is really a chicken, she reflected. She put the potatoes in the frying pan, diced, because that's how Cloe liked them. She lowered the heat, shook the pan vigorously, stirred the potatoes and seasoned them with salt and pepper. She hated the feel of metal on her lips. Once the potatoes were crunchy, the way her younger daughter liked them, Nora added four beaten eggs. She performed these actions without thinking, mechanically. Are you sure you're not running late? asked one of the minichefs with red ears and a white hat. It was what the taxi driver with the two surnames would have said. Only one is real. My name is Paul Smith Page. Her thoughts moved to bamboo structures; the oldest one, in Manchuria, was three thousand years old. The buildings are resilient, in the event of an earthquake they move with the ground. Grandfather always talked about the structures, not the cladding. If a bamboo structure is well made it's practically everlasting.

I'm not coming in the end, I'm staying at Pau's. Who was this Pau? Nora told her daughter that the potato omelette would be just as good for breakfast or lunch the next day. Mamà, who do you take me for? There's no way I'll be there for breakfast. Maybe lunch? The stabilizers had come off her little girl's bicycle aeons ago. She could have ruminated for hours about this Pau character and her little Cloe, but she was distracted by a text message she'd just received. Dinner at my place; not in Pedralbes, in Sant Pol. Had she read it correctly? Now Nacho was inviting her to his place, with no third wheel? Completely normal. She thought about structures again. I shall be structure. I'll offer him only the cladding, he'll never touch the frame again.

While she drove, she thought of the five plane trees on the promenade in front of her beach apartment. One January morning some men had come to prune them. They pruned two of the trees, one tall and strong, with a massive trunk, and a smaller one next to it, young but also strong. The other three they'd cut down to stumps. Nora was intrigued by worms, those tiny bodies that wriggled along. One of the trees was rotten, that's why they'd cut it down, but what about the other two?

In the spring, Nora liked to drive with the top down and feel the wind in her face; it was like swimming in the sea in the middle of December. She was driving up the Maresme coast, and although she'd made a conscious decision to be only cladding, she felt more alive than she had in years. What awaited her in Sant Pol? There was no point lying to herself: she couldn't wait to see him. She arrived at a little white house by the sea. There was a terrace on the first floor, where a table had been laid with a linen tablecloth, candles, open oysters, and sea urchin au gratin. White wine. He'd cooked the sea urchin like that, stuffed, especially for her. I know you like them. They smiled, he with his eyes. It made her think of Bogart, like that first time at the airport. The chairs on the terrace were dark wood, the table too. She moved slowly.

'We could go live in a bamboo house,' she said.

'Sorry?'

'Let's talk about the game.'

'What game?'

'Nacho, stop pretending.'

'Not now. We're together now. Better not to talk about that.'

'Why not?'

'Sometimes it's best not to know certain things.'

'But I want to know.' Her gaze was fixed on a purple-tipped urchin.

'No you don't.' He couldn't take his eyes off her, that woman had captivated him.

'Bamboo structures move with the ground when there's an earthquake.'

Nora thought of her grandfather and his motto: be yourself! She didn't know why she was the way she was. She was still looking at the sea urchin, it really did have purple spines. The colourful ones are male, the edible ones; the black ones with longer spikes are female. The females are poisonous. As she thought about this, she rubbed the index finger and thumb of her left hand together, both of which had had urchin tips lodged in them since childhood. She'd been pricked by them several times. Her grandfather had always removed the spines, but on that particular day Nora had wanted them to stay lodged in her finger. Grandfather—don't. If I keep them forever, then you'll always be with me. It had worked.

Nora couldn't stop thinking about the game they were playing. She couldn't forget that this man had turned her into a whore and that she'd allowed it. But she didn't want to bring it up again. They were all right now. They would go on playing, Nacho thought, but only for a while longer. After the exhibition, he'd put an end to it. Women always wanted him to hold them. With Nora, for the first time, it was he who wanted something. He'd just realised that he needed her. He hadn't needed anyone since his mother. He was no longer the king of pain, he was starting to feel like the ruler of a kingdom inhabited only by the two of them. He was afraid of losing her, but for the first time in his life it was a risk he was prepared to take.

'The meaning of some of the paintings can't be conveyed through words,' Nora said. 'I think my exhibition will surprise you. I know it will. When I love you always means something else, that's the title I've chosen.'

'When I love you?'

'When I love you always means something else.'

'And what does that mean?'

'I don't know. You've never said *I love you* to me.'

'You haven't either. I want to read you a story ... let's go up to the roof for a while.'

The white house had a rooftop, from which you could view the water and the seagulls. They lay down on a mattress, holding hands, naked under the blankets, gazing at the sky. Nora thought of the seagull-dog, the water, the woman who was pissed off with the foreigners. No games. She felt good with him, comfortable, fully herself in a way that was new. But he'd mucked things up. They moved to Nacho's library, a large room lined with books, books and a fireplace. Nora reclined, naked, on a chaise longue. He licked the big toe of her left foot, then sat down in a nearby armchair. He read to her from Hemingway's *The Old Man at the Bridge* while she watched him. She listened to his voice laden with magnetism. She thought of another old man, not her grandfather, but the hunched, white-haired man at the entrance of a local bookstore. What is he waiting for? For the woman he loves to come in. He looks scruffy, a bit barmy, and yet a girl loved him once. That happened long ago, but he is still waiting for her.

'I'm scared of dying,' Nora said. 'There's so much that happens after you're gone.' She was thinking of her parents and what they had missed. Somehow, she felt comfortable talking to this man who had betrayed her, it was as if she were talking to herself. But she didn't want to get hooked, he'd used her, and love was no longer an option. She still felt the same way about him, she still wanted him, but she was resolved to ignore her feelings. Her heart would not be broken.

'I'm not afraid of dying. What I'm scared of is not understanding reality, seeing something and not knowing what it is, not being able to decipher it.' That's what he said, and it felt like a confession he'd never made to anyone. What terrified him was never understanding why his mother had to die.

That night they made love like a normal couple, however normal couples make love. There were no third parties, no tatamis, no acne-ridden youths. They loved each other. She promised herself it would be the last time she would love him. He told himself that this woman would be his, that he would always love her. He had conjured her up after one of his street fights in Segovia when he was young. He gazed at her, asleep on her side, head pillowed on her arm, and thought it was for her that he'd come to blows with those guys he disliked, he had brawled for her, though he hadn't met her yet. It didn't matter, since his mother's death he'd earned the right to clash with whomever he pleased, for whatever reason. He hadn't even known her then! So what? He dreamt up what he wanted, when he wanted. And Nora traversed the skies in the arms of the man she was in love with, but who had betrayed her. We're just part of the supporting cast here, all of us. The only one who knows anything is the prompter. She was pretending to be asleep. She had a right to live, she had a right to her new kingdom. And every day there were more and more seagulls in town.

19

SOMETIMES SHE FELT LIKE SHE DIDN'T KNOW WHERE SHE WAS. She wondered if it was all really happening. But there was no evidence to indicate it wasn't. She'd avoided phoning Júlia for days, because when she did everything became all too real. Júlia had told her to break it off, she'd said it wasn't right ... that wasn't what she'd meant when she spoke of infidelity. Ah, so now, to top things off, I need to be unfaithful the way you want me to be! Nora had yelled before hanging up on her. She needed to tell someone about what she was going through, but there was no one. The people who would have listened without judging were dead, and Robert obviously wasn't an option. Teresa, her therapist, had passed away. She ended up talking to a street cleaner one day, and she felt better afterwards. The woman listened to her with a smile while she was sweeping up the muck on the pavement. Nora had walked to the recycling bins and the woman was there with her gentle laugh. They greeted each other and Nora told her everything: the plane, the earrings, the perils of swearing eternal love, the dead Countess of Segovia,

Tatami Man with his hairy hands, the silly, spotty boy and her other customers, the dinner in Sant Pol, her own artwork. The fact that I love you always means something else. The street cleaner nodded. When they parted, the woman waved to her from across the street and shouted, It always means something else!

Despite her determination not to love Nacho, with him Nora felt alive. You and I are as one, that's what she would have wished to tell him if he had acted differently. Both of them had lived through unusually painful circumstances at a young age. They were so different that someone might mistake one for the other. The radio—how she hated her husband's preferred method of waking up. She let him hug her: the heat from his body had the same effect on her as tyre rubber. The financial problems of Senyor Attorney's law firm were beginning to affect their relationship and this weighed on Nora. If something isn't working, you change it, complaining is useless. He joked that she'd end up with her own Lonelyhearts show on the radio. *What's troubling you, dear friend? You can speak openly here. We listen but never judge, we'll help you find the best way out of your problems. We peddle solutions—joy!* That good and gentle man was growing bitter, losing the plot. *Bon dia*, Nora said as she turned over to face him. She'd stroked that face all her life and yet this morning it was as if she were seeing him for the first time. Now that she thought that things with Nacho were coming to an end, she felt repulsed by Robert.

'Not doing so great, actually', he said as he removed her

hands from his face and took them in his. She was just as beautiful now as she'd been as a girl.

'You can't go on like this day after day.'

'And what do you suggest I do?'

'Find a solution.'

'Easy for you to say, painting all day long!'

'What is that supposed to mean? You know I try to help you as much as I can.'

'Sure, sure.'

It was as if some other person were speaking for him. He'd been moody lately and she didn't understand why. He flew off the handle, making everyone angry with him and with each other. He longed for something different. He wasn't sure what was troubling him at times, he thought it was one thing when in fact it was the opposite, or maybe not the opposite but something else entirely. He often felt he was sucking dry the very souls of those he loved. Now more than ever. What on earth was he doing?

'When you come from factory people, the slate is wiped clean after each death.' That's how it came out, what she said.

'Sorry?'

To make matters worse, Nora was unfazed, she always stood by him. He would have preferred for her to shout at him and tell him he was useless, that he was mucking everything up, for her to tell him off or casually let him know, as if it were nothing, that she'd fallen in love with someone else. There were so many men out there who could make her happy. But she wouldn't do that. She'd loved him since she was a girl, and Nora believed in those she loved. Júlia always said it: Nora makes the people she loves feel important. So, what on earth was he doing?

'It's just something Grandfather used to say,' Nora said.

'Right, and now I suppose you'll remind me of how the great Hemingway built an empire out of nothing. Yes, I know, we should all be grateful. He was perfect, the rest of us not so much. A born winner who rose out of poverty.'

'Grandfather was my everything.' Nora didn't feel guilty for cheating on Robert with another man. Or maybe she should use the plural? She couldn't understand why, but it was a fact.

'I know. You and your grandfather ...'

'Robert, what's wrong? You're so resentful! I paint because it's the only thing I know how to do, you know that better than anyone. You know my story, what I am and what I am not. You know where I come from, what I come from, who I grew up with.'

'I'm losing it all ... everything I am, everything I have.'

'Robert, what are you talking about?' He was miserable, and she couldn't help him.

'Forget it, don't mind me. Sorry. I'm not handling things well at the moment. There's so much you don't know ...' He stood by the bed, having put on a pair of neatly-pressed trousers, and looked his wife in the eye.

'What do you mean?' Robert was a good man. He'd always loved her, protected her. And how did she repay him? She was just trying to hang on, that was all. If Nacho wasn't in the picture, she and Robert might not even be together. It's thanks to the lover that a marriage survives. She'd read that somewhere.

'Your grandfather's phrase, it's not bad', Robert said while putting on a black shirt he couldn't remember buying. 'When you're poor, the slate is wiped clean after each death.'

If Robert got a spot on his clothes at a business lunch, he'd often just walk into a store, throw away the stained garment, and buy a new one. Nora was amused by this at first, then she found it stupid, then, over time, she stopped noticing. Everything comes to an end, more so in a relationship that lasts many years. The family is the hand that pushes the head underwater, a poet friend had once told her.

'And when you're not poor as well,' Nora added with that tight-lipped expression of hers.

'Why does laundry detergent always smell of fish?' Robert sniffed his shirt sleeve and breathed in. He laughed.

'Now I understand why cats always chase after you,' Nora said.

They looked at each other for the first time. A few seconds later they both laughed. That was something, those two sentences, they'd said when they were young. Their laughter broke the tension.

'What are we going to do?' Robert said. 'The law firm is failing, only Maria and I are left, and if things don't improve I'll have to let her go, too.'

Robert was opening up to her for the first time in days. Nora knelt on the bed and hugged him. He kissed her on the forehead.

'You'll pull through, you always have.' She caressed his head. 'I'll help you in any way I can.'

'I don't want your help! I need to do this on my own.'

Her comment had been the wrong thing to say; the thought of Nora helping him was distressing to Robert.

'And you always have, Robert! You've always managed to

pull through on your own.'

'Yes, but it's not working this time.'

'It will ... you know what my secret is?' Nora stretched out on the bed again.

'Yes, making love to Leonard Cohen,' he said in a tired voice.

Having uttered this last sentence Robert left the room, then the house. Still on the bed, Nora heard the garage door open, the sound of the car engine start up, and the door close again with a sharp bang. She wasn't concerned about the law firm, but the man was losing his sense of humour and *that* was worrying. A white smock with nothing underneath; Nora was naked, and so was the canvas. Everything else receded. She painted because she didn't want to see things as they were but as they should be. The *St. Matthew Passion* was playing. She'd noticed that Robert was acting strange, but she wasn't sure it was all work related. The bit about the firm didn't bother her, and the show would be a success, she could feel it. She always withdrew from the world when she was preparing an exhibition. Robert had known that for years. Who could tell what was going through that man's head! His wife had stopped being faithful after a lifetime together, and all he could think about was the office. Didn't he realise? Nora was seeking relief from her dull married life. She painted herself with her customers. Maybe he did sense something, but Nora didn't want to think about it; they had lived separate lives for too long already. She painted nonstop. And fucked once a week, always with a different customer. Acrylic dries fast, it's water-based and odourless. She painted with acrylic so she could smell the tyre rubber. If she'd used oil-based paint the tyre smell would have been masked, and without the smell of rubber the world as she knew it would cease to exist. She was putting the finishing touches to her last painting. The paint brushes had become an extension of her body. She herself was a brush. The exhibition opened in three weeks.

Through her art work, she could change the channels in her mind and make the whole universe disappear. Growing old was that, she thought, losing people. Nora had started to grow old at a young age. In the end she'd lost her grandfather as well. All she had left was Robert, and he was starting to look like a cheap version of himself. But, with Nacho and her customers she felt alive. Always a new customer, a one-time thing. She felt like a woman, a real woman with voluptuous breasts and body. Pain and fulfilment often touch each other. She was devastated when she realised Nacho was using her as his whore, but the pain had opened up a new world for her, turning desire into a calling. He knew things about her that she herself did not, but he didn't know what she knew. To love someone is to love the truest version of themselves: I know you and love you as you are. She would have wanted to be that way with Nacho, but she didn't know how. Everything we know of love we know by having cared for just a few people. Thus, we are limited: the love of a few people, certain faces we hold dear. That's all we can do. Who could behold and love all people, all faces, at the same time? A love whore. Nora had decided to follow desire wherever it led her. She would choose risk over the daily grind. It wasn't that she was dead before, but she hadn't been alive either. She was now though, and one day she'd be gone. It was fine. For the first time, Madame Bovary didn't strike her as silly. She must have been lonely.

A woman conjures love to give herself the means to satisfy her thirst for it. Nora had read that somewhere. Perhaps she'd invented Nacho in order to become a prostitute and deliver herself from her own prisons. Maybe Nacho had just been an excuse, and it could have been anyone. Love intensified pleasure in a way that seemed disproportionate, that went beyond someone's flaws and qualities. And the seagulls, what about them? That taxi driver would never be a customer of hers, but she'd paint him today, his face and hands would appear in the background of her latest creation.

The hardest thing about painting with acrylic was creating volume. And rhythm. It was like a quick, loveless fuck. Sex for the sake of sex. Wasn't that also a form of love? She thought about the frescoes she'd seen with her grandfather. They were mostly lime plaster-based, the colours were made from mineral and vegetable powders to which water was added; pigments made with a type of oil were used later. Oil adds volume and allows you to work the paint more. But, she'd learned to paint in her grandfather's office using acrylics so as not to disturb him with the smell of turpentine. She thought about the first famous oil painting, she couldn't remember the title, but it was of some Flemish count-dukes, by Van Eyck. I was born dead, Nacho had told her.

20

EVERYTHING WAS READY, ONLY THE PEOPLE, THE ACTORS, were missing. How can you achieve timeless sculptures when these are living beings? Since she was a teenager she'd wavered between thinking that most people were complete bastards or that the world was filled with kind-hearted souls. She felt good in that bright place, tucked away in the forests of Montjuïc. Forty large format paintings. Often she didn't trust her own judgement, but that wasn't the case that day. Early summer. The air translucent. Fewer people in the city. The silence in the room was so great you could almost hear it. A few hours later the noise would be real. Nora didn't know what death was, no one does until they experience it. But she did know what it was like to live through the death of others. One day she would weep for all of them. You're hiding something aren't you? She put on Beethoven's *Clair de Lune* and glanced at her feet. Those sandals made her even taller. Black dress. Bengali shawl. The lady who made it spent months embroidering the orange silk fabric. Nora had hardly taken it off since Júlia gave it to her. Especially in the summer. It made her feel safe. She was also wearing her countess earrings. As she looked around at the paintings, she thought about her customers during those last six months: the Tatami Mans, the silly, spotty boy, the one who talked nonstop and didn't dare touch her, the one who wanted to do it on a bed of uncooked rice, the banker, the one who could only come if he had cherries in his mouth ... Only one go, only one night. There was even a man who'd never been anyone's customer before. Nora's loose hair fell to her waist.

We're all here to be spectators, the problem is most of us have turned into actors. She thought of the Benedictine monks who invented champagne. Their first rule: listen! Júlia arrived early, wearing gladiator sandals and a sheer dress that accentuated her still-perfect breasts. She was accompanied by yet another young boyfriend, more attract-ive than ever, and his camera. You look absolutely radiant, great shawl! Júlia said as she hugged her. She circled the room and declared: You'll sell them all today, so I want one—now! Júlia didn't know it, because they'd stopped discussing 'the matter', but the painting she chose was of her young photographer. His camera didn't figure in the composition.

Her daughters arrived with their dates. Pau was now Cloe's official boyfriend. Mom, the little red elves in our kitchen told me—he's a keeper! she'd said breathlessly. Well if the little elves told you ... Lluc and Pau looked at Nora as if she was a Greek goddess and kissed her on both cheeks. Congratulations on your show! Pau said, blushing. What had her daughters told them about her? Nora glanced at the four of them and smiled: they looked like they had just stepped out of a summer ad campaign. Seemingly perfect. Sorry, what was that? The people in the paintings ... they're all naked, Jana said.

It was getting crowded, and Nora had to attend to potential buyers. The shy publisher had just approached her, they hadn't spoken in months, not since their last phone call. You look beautiful, the work is outstanding! I'd love for you to illustrate a new book for me. The man never went with hookers, Nora had no doubt about it, but was he always so very bland, didn't he ever speak out of turn? That was all Nora could think. Painting pictures and shagging strangers was her life now. Thank you, she said. There were too many people there, it was hard to move around. Robert, however, was missing. It was the first time he'd been late to an exhibition of hers. They hadn't watched *The Blue Angel* or anything else after London, that's how things stood. They didn't listen to each other, didn't even notice each other. All that about the fragility of life didn't seem so irrelevant now. They were no longer the movers and shakers. Robert didn't understand her, he'd forgotten they could descend into the depths of hell, which was exactly what had happened. He no longer protected her from the pain underlying all things, no longer wondered about the secrets she held in her heart. He was a sad imitation of who he'd once been.

Nacho approached and Nora was suffused by the same warmth as always. Even now that she'd decided to leave him, it still happened. You're wearing the countess earrings. I am. I bought one of your paintings. Which one? The woman with the blue face. Why did you paint her face blue? I'm not sure.

She noticed that Nacho was looking at her differently. As if he'd just invented her, as if no one had ever looked at her before. You're *good*, Nora. Have dinner with me later. I'm not sure. Nacho wasn't himself that night either. She'd noticed the change when they had supper at his house. She thought about the Coca-Cola lorry she'd seen parked by the art gallery, on the front of which was written LOVES, plural.

It was the point in the show when you wander through the crowd catching snippets of conversation. If he could only play the accordion well he'd be Piazzolla and famous; Bertolucci offered him the soundtrack to *Last Tango in Paris* but he turned him down because he had some concerts lined up, so he gave it to Gato Barbieri, an absolute idiot, and he became famous instead. That was what three middle-aged couples were talking about, as they stood transfixed in front of a painting one of the wives wanted to buy to hang above the sofa in her living room. The lady's eyes were trained on the jerking foot of one of the men, not her husband, and the man was looking at her. When the whole world sings and sings badly, in the end the last man standing is the worst singer. This last sentence was spoken by an Argentine gallery owner, bald and overweight, who was talking to his much younger boyfriend, a slim bloke from Galicia. They were referring to Andrés Calamaro's *El cantante*. The younger man liked the song but the Argentinean said Calamaro was terrible, had a nasal voice, he couldn't stand him, he reminded him of too many things he wished to forget. The Argentine was the most influential gallerist in Santander. Nora, *mi amor*, this is exactly what I want for my gallery.

You're going to sell everything tonight, so you'll have to put something together just for me. Nora nodded. You'll have it. You look divine as always, and where is that gorgeous husband of yours? I have no idea, she said as she moved away. Then she spotted Robert coming in. Her heart didn't skip a beat, no sudden warmth suffused her body. They were both taller than most people, so in a sea of heads they could always spot each other.

'You're wearing your Portobello earrings!'

'Yes, and you, what have you been up to?'

'They look great on you.'

'Thanks. Did something happen? You're late.'

'You'll always be the most beautiful woman at the party and you know it.'

They didn't say anything else, and Nora let it drop. After twenty-five years she knew when her husband didn't want to talk. She watched as he wandered off with a group of lawyer friends, she had time to catch a few of their sentences. Your wife has outdone herself yet again, said a magistrate from Girona who'd been on TV recently because of a high-profile corruption case; he was your average handsome bloke with horn-rimmed glasses. She's fantastic, isn't she, she heard Robert reply mechanically, as if it had nothing to do with him. As if being her husband was a drag. You're lucky, she still looks smashing! Yes, she's the best, all around, always the best. He said it in a way that showed his fatigue. The fragility of life—they were the embodiment of that now. More and more red dots appeared on the paintings that hung on those white walls. The show was going well. She'd kill a papaya tree of thirst in the middle of a river. The rude remark was made by a Colombian friend of hers in reference to an ugly woman; he was addressing three young girls who were hanging on his every word as if he were some kind of guru. He tossed out comments like that and the girls laughed. Nora had often heard him reel off those worn-out lines. One of the girls was sure to fall for it that night, of this Nora was certain, maybe even all three of them would. She knew he liked to have more than one woman at a time. The unrestrained laughter of a woman is the gateway to sex, the Colombian always said. Yes, no doubt all three of them would be reeled in like fish. Poor things, they always developed a crush on him and then he wanted nothing more to do with them. Another red dot, and another. Bryan Ferry had the ability only the English possess of turning the tackiest thing into something classy. She had to agree with this last statement. There was a time, when the girls were little, when they listened to Avalon all the time. When I love you always means something else. What a great title! she heard Júlia exclaim to her toyboy. He was about as young as Lluc and somewhat taller than Cloe's elf-endorsed Pau. The crowd was starting to thin out.

Nora would have liked to leave. People exhausted her. At that moment she was thinking that her mother's heart had given out so that Grandfather would never be able to forgive himself. Her mother had died so that her grandfather would forever be filled with self-hatred, and she'd succeeded. Her grandfather, for all his apparent strength, never forgave himself. He didn't forgive himself for any of the three deaths, or for what he'd done to her. People really tired Nora. The most influential art critics in the country, journalists, celebrities and lawyers, gallerists from all over Spain and some from abroad had all attended the opening. It was nice, but she'd had enough. Nora was shy and not very demonstrative, she had trouble expressing herself and always seemed to be gazing off in another direction. She could only look the people she loved in the eye. Success overwhelmed her. She ventured over to Robert, wishing to find her old husband again. Usually he was able to help. Her husband had a way with people, he made a good first impression, knew how to engage in small talk. But this time she'd been left to her own devices.

'Come and give me a hug,' she told him when there was almost no one left in the room. 'Are you happy for me?'

'You succeed and I fail,' was all he said as he embraced her and planted one of those kisses on her forehead. Then he turned and headed for the exit.

I'm not feeling too well, he'd said, I think I'll take a walk. You do your thing, have dinner with whoever you need to have dinner with. I'll see you at home. And congratulations on the exhibition, what a success, you sold all your paintings! Nora watched him wending his way across the room. Her husband wasn't the same, his arms hung loose at his sides, his broad shoulders looked narrow. Before he was out of sight she called to him: We're still going strong, Robert, we're still the same! He turned his head and gave a reluctant half-smile. Not even she believed it. Everything had changed, little by little at first, then suddenly at the speed of light. We don't really know how we lose the important people in our lives; it doesn't happen overnight but in tiny increments, over a long period of time. One morning, any morning, one of the two says, It's over. Growing old is too painful. She still loved him, but they were no longer the same people. Robert didn't understand what all those nudes were about, those naked women in obscene poses. They reminded him of something that made him uncomfortable, but he didn't want to ask about it.

Robert said nothing more, he just walked out the door. Nora was left alone, and then that Bogart smile suddenly appeared in front of her. Nacho had stayed until the end. He'd bought one of her paintings, the woman with the blue face. The man who'd used her was changing too, maybe something was going on with him as well. Robert had left without noticing that Nacho was still there. The three of them had been practically alone in the room and nothing had happened. At another point in their lives her husband would have become territorial and defended what was his. Now he didn't even notice the tomcat that wanted to steal his mate.

'Nora, if you didn't exist I'd have to create you.'

'I'm just an invention.'

'I know. Dinner?'

'Let's.'

'How did you ever come up with a naked blue-faced woman and a man licking her breasts?'

'It came to me in a dream.'

'My father saw everything in a positive light, it really irritated me after my mother died.'

'Your mother died?'

'When I was six. My father used to say: We all do what we can. But no, far from it! In general, there are those who do what they can but only a few who do what needs to be done, and if that means they are screwed, so be it. I was like that, I tried to do what should be done, until my mother died with a blue face in the arms of a stranger who was licking her breasts. That's what I was like before, and what I want to be again, with you. With you, I want to do what should be done.'

Nora froze. 'Like in my painting?'

'Sorry?'

'The blue face. It's like my painting.'

'Yes.'

'And who decides what needs to be done?'

'You do!'

Now he was courting her, but it was too late.

'Shall we find a place to eat?' she said, looking at the man with a blue-faced dead mother, the man who had hurt her.

It was his deepest secret. Nacho had just shared his truth with her, the thing that made him a survivor. She had painted the picture some time earlier and now it was his, it belonged to the only man she'd ever been in love with. We compete in order to learn to cooperate so that we can compete again. She remembered Joyce Pensato and her Donald Duck-filled studio, so cold in winter. Nora lived in a scruffy grey parka, a flask stuffed in her pocket. They were in Brooklyn, and Joyce could drop in for dinner any day.

21

NORA TOLD HIM SHE'D BEEN MEASURING THE PASSAGE OF time since the death of her mastiff, Aton. Time can be calculated conventionally or by taking the life of a dog as a unit of measurement. They were at the oyster restaurant in Sarrià, sitting outside. Nacho was looking at her in that new way of his that was beginning to trouble her. She preferred the man who had used her rather than the man with those puppy eyes. Now she was the one who was closed off. The oyster is difficult to open because it's a wounded animal furiously protecting itself. What can I get you? asked the Brazilian server, who spoke Catalan with a sexy accent. Any job can be done with excellence: for years João had lived up to her grandfather's maxim. He'd been Júlia's lover for a few months, and now Nora was imagining him as a customer, though he didn't look like the kind of man who'd pay to be told he is desired. Nora had a married friend who went whoring, though not very often, and she preferred not to hear about it; she'd always been disgusted by men who used prostitutes and then told you about it. She remembered

Salva's words. I don't get it, Nora, when I'm with a prostitute she comes in five minutes, always, but there are times when I spend more than an hour with Maria and nothing happens. Nora didn't say anything. Poor Maria! While she was caught up in these thoughts, Nacho placed their order with the waiter.

He'd asked for oysters and a nice white wine. João brought out slices of buttered rye bread to go with them. The square was filled with children trailing a young couple who were making soap bubbles. The girl was wearing a white tutu with a black vest and a wig with red feathers. A crescent moon and two stars were painted on her face. She was thin, her collarbone protruded. He had a green clown nose, a black top hat, sunglasses. She blew medium-sized bubbles, he made giant ones, and the children chased them round the square. Some of the bubbles soared above the trees, and Nora followed them with her eyes until they burst. On a night like that, by the light of the street lamps and the full moon, the soap bubbles glimmered. The couple had a hungry-looking dog with black and white spots, and a music box that played the theme song from *Amélie*.

'You know we have lives of our own, but we're also part of something bigger?' Nacho said. She'd heard him say that before, Nora thought as her eyes followed a giant bubble rising above a blue rooftop. 'I don't believe in God, but I do believe in the church, the building itself though, its stones.' And she'd heard that sentence more than once too. So what? Nacho was spewing empty words, empty because he hadn't loved her, he'd just used her. He'd made a beautiful bubble and then he'd burst it. What did he want now? She remembered the day Cloe had asked her who the gods were. They talked about it a bit and then her daughter said, I think a bottle of water turned into a god and that's why the sea is blue. Nora smiled at the thought of seven-year-old Cloe discovering the world. 'I've told you about my pain. I've never shared that with anyone before,' he said.

'I appreciate that you've shared your truth with me, but you've also turned me into a whore ... do you always have to talk this way? Frankly, I don't know if I'm keeping a secret. I have no idea. But you've turned me into what I am now, and I allowed it. I'm sorry about your mother, but that doesn't give you the right to treat other women like pieces of meat. Do you know why I allowed you to use me? Because I was in love with you, I wanted you, whatever the price. I didn't understand it at first, it wasn't until that young guy, the one in the photos, with the spots ... and then I let myself be used, as punishment for being so stupid, for having loved you. I fell in love. I loved you!'

'That's over. From now on it's just you and me.'

'Maybe it's over for you, but I'm still there, fucking your one-time clients. You can't turn a woman into a whore and then expect her to stop overnight because that's what you want, because you've suddenly realised something. And what have you realised? That you love me?'

'Yes, I love you ... So, do you have an outward gaze or inward?'

'I don't know. Does it bear any relevance to being a whore? Could you please stop speaking in platitudes and look at me!'

'It always matters.'

Maybe they shared the fact they were both hiding a deep

pain, that was a natural connection, but he'd betrayed her, and for Nora there was no turning back. Love doesn't judge, her mother had once told her. But pain does, she thought, betrayal even more so. Now she knew what Nacho meant when he talked about deep pain, and there was something else she'd discovered over the last few months, something she'd never experienced before: the pain of giving yourself to another only to be betrayed. They'd finished their oysters. Soap bubbles were still floating in the air. The girl in the wig with red feathers had a glittering teardrop tattoo under her right eye. Nora had been afraid of suffering, she'd always pushed pain away, out of sight. But when it came to Nacho she hadn't been in control, she'd let go, removed her armour, and he hadn't even noticed. She'd given him the most genuine part of herself and he'd stabbed her with a dagger. Now she knew she could survive without any armour. If she was wounded by another dagger, she would rip it out, suck the blood, lick her wound. Nacho continued to caress her hand. When you've been stabbed, the pain doesn't allow you to feel much else. They were silent, both caught up in their own thoughts. Again Nora remembered what the visual artist from New York had said. We compete with each other in order to learn to cooperate, so that we can compete again. Joyce Pensato was her name.

'Nowadays, when I swim underwater I end up thinking someone might catch me like a fish,' Nacho said absentmindedly.

'I always dive in naked, with my mouth open,' she said, 'and lately a hook seems to snag me by the tongue, the underside, and pulls me out of the water. Up, up. When you're caught in the sea you always go up.'

'You know what that means?' he asked, as his index finger continued to draw circles in the palm of Nora's hand.

'A lie.' She withdrew her hand.

'Nora, the game's over, I'll make it up to you.'

'Sure you will. Is that what pimps say to their whores?'

'Look at me!'

'I looked at you once ...' she said, her eyes still on the bubble-dancer's teardrop tattoo. 'Now I'm thinking about the air vents on cars.'

'What?'

'It's such a shoddy design. Where exactly are the vents that are meant to control the airflow inside?'

'They're in the front, underneath,' Nacho said.

'Exactly. And similarly the exhaust pipe is placed at the back. But that's designed as if cars are alone on the road, it doesn't take into account the fact that we spend our days following other cars, in the city, on the road. We all absorb the fumes from other cars' combustion, in a long crappy chain. We've created a system of dependency where no one breathes their own air anymore. We need to regulate the location of air vents, they should be placed on the roof, like in amphibious all-terrain vehicles. I need my own air to live. And you?'

Nora realised it had been months since she'd had a whiff of rubber, she still carried a piece of it in her bag.

Nacho didn't say anything, he didn't give a damn about air vents, his eyes were on Nora's lips. They wouldn't be making love today, Nora had made that clear, but he never tired of looking at her. It had been months since she'd smelled the piece of rubber in her bag, hadn't touched it either, or at least he hadn't caught her doing so for quite a while. He noticed her lucent pupils; until now they'd been lifeless, vacant. She was coming back to life. She'd broken the mother of all taboos, she was brave, and this made her powerful in his eyes. He tried to remember the times they'd been together and he'd taken them for granted. Now he'd kill to be with her again, the way they were before. That night her mind was especially sharp. Nora was very feminine, but she had a strong masculine side to her as well. He still didn't know her pain, what had happened to her.

For years Nora's goal in life had been to go unnoticed, but this wasn't a concern of hers anymore. She'd always prioritised life, the facticity of being alive, over her pain, her feelings. She never cried because crying was pointless, crying was for idiots. Almost everyone she'd loved had died. So what? Why should she weep? If you can't do anything about it, then put it behind you and move on. If she hadn't cried when faced with these losses, she certainly wouldn't now. She was alive and the man sitting in front of her had wounded her, but he hadn't broken her. She liked her present life and what she was in the process of discovering. The show had gone well, she felt liberated, like a great weight had been lifted, though she didn't know exactly why. Her husband was acting more and more strange and she didn't care. The man sitting in front of her, for whom she would have killed a few months before, wanted her madly now and that too left her cold. It amused her. She'd never sat down to dinner after a show with such a feeling of calm. Suddenly she remembered that line from *Simon of the Desert*: you have to stick it out until the end. Simon, the Christian ascetic who'd climbed atop a column and began to preach. Simon the Stylite. In the film, Silvia Pinal, a Mexican actress with enormous breasts, appears to Simon of the Desert in multiple forms, including as a female incarnation of the devil. The Sinai desert ... . At the end of the movie there's a flash forward. Simon of the Desert is now a modern character, an intellectual. Sick of being at a nightclub, he tells the woman he's with that he wants to leave. Her reply: *Hay que aguantar hasta el final.*

vehicle. The doors and windows were shut, but a glimmer of light was visible through the cracks. When she was almost there she heard music. She opened the window and saw a dancing clown with a gold ball in each hand. The balls were like the ones on the railing at the beach apartment. She felt like she was dreaming someone else's dream. Behind him was a sign that read: *Dancin' Clown*. The familiar song ended and started again. But the clown was just part of the decor. The important thing was that Nora was swimming like a fish now, circling the clown, naked, with her silver chain and those black hearts on her nipples, and a shark was hugging her with its fins and licking her, a great white shark. She wasn't afraid. She kissed it. Little by little it turned into a sea bream, and Nora's limbs began to dissolve, her teeth grew larger, and she started growing white fins. The song was coming to an end, it slowed and became crackly. Then it stopped completely, Nora realised she was no longer herself, she was eating the sea bream, no longer kissing it but devouring it and taking pleasure in it. She was huge and white.

Sandra was knocking on her bedroom door. Senyora, someone has sent you some flowers. May I come in? Yes, of course. Sandra had worked for her for twenty-four years, her hair was thin now, balding in spots. She smiled as she walked towards the bed holding a bouquet of white roses. I counted sixty-nine of them! They're beautiful, and there's a note. Her ankles were swollen, her skin was dry. I'll leave them right here, at the foot of the bed. Nora sat up, covering her naked body with the linen sheet, caressing her breast. She opened the envelope. It occurred to her that one day her ankles

22

THE CLOUDS WERE IN THE SHAPE OF TASMANIA. SHE'D dreamed about the campervan again, but now it was intact. She looked at the sky and sat up so she could see the city: the sight of it was reassuring. She was at home and Nacho had disappeared. The dream began with a shark and a sea bream kissing underwater. The shark had the body of a man and the sea bream that of a woman. The male body was younger than the female, it was particularly noticeable in the arms. They swam toward each other from a distance of about six metres and when their lips touched they smiled with their eyes. Behind them, only the deep water, and in the middle of nowhere the trailer with the word RAINBOW all lit up. The letters were familiar, they were like the calligraphy she did on ruled paper when she was a schoolgirl. She'd once written an entire love letter to her grandfather in that simple cursive. Grandfather, you and I will always be together. You and I will never be eaten by sharks. Much less by a great white shark. I promise. I won't let you down. You'll see. The shark and the bream disappeared. Nora walked toward the would look like Sandra's. Inside was a cheque for a large sum of money, and a note. *Nora, it's over. I hope you will forgive me. I want to end the game, I want us to start a life together. I've transferred the business to a Russian guy.*

She took a deep breath. The dream had rattled her, all that stuff about being a shark that was eating a bream with a man's head. The bream had Nacho's face. And now the letter, the cheque, the white roses. She took another deep breath. *I believe in coincidences. There's a song that's been with me since I was thirteen. I heard it on the seventh anniversary of my mother's death and immediately identified with it. I'd had this sense of abandonment since her passing, ever since the terrible day of her death, her blue face. The King of Pain—that was me. Since then, in my dreams I've often encountered a rich man sleeping in a gold bed, a seagull with a broken back, a mottled sun, a salmon frozen in a waterfall, a skeleton choking on a breadcrumb, one of my hats high up in a tree ... and the inescapable fate of being the king of pain forever.*

Her breathing had slowed again. She liked full-bodied wines, the ones that are made with the grape skins. She would pour herself a glass before she read any more. She tiptoed downstairs in her ripped T-shirt and black cotton knickers, hoping she wouldn't run into anyone in the kitchen. It was relaxing to feel the parquet under her bare feet, but as she opened the refrigerator the cold tiles in the kitchen made her shiver. Her feet were cold. She poured herself a glass of wine and hurried upstairs. The feel of wood once again. Back in bed she glanced at the letter, the cream-coloured paper against the white sheets, the neat, round handwriting almost like a rebuke. It reminded her of the girls at school who had rectangular pencil cases with coloured pens and underlined sections of their notes in different colours. She removed her T-shirt. Naked, she lay next to the letter with her arms crossed. She felt the same as when she floated on her back in the sea. The alcohol helped her forget. She resumed reading, still lying down, holding the letter up in front of her eyes. *Yesterday in the car, on the way up to Sant Pol, I put the CD on. I still love 'King of Pain', but I no longer feel like the king of pain. It's true. I've left that kingdom for the one we built together without even realising we were. A kingdom so vast it can accommodate everything, yet so small there's only room for the two of us, so beautiful that others aren't able to see it, as indestructible as the strongest woman and man: you and me. And in that place I am with you as I have never been before. My mother is a beautiful memory and a painful one, but it no longer tortures me. I can finally live and love. I'm free. Let's end the game. I want to be with you, Nora.*

Without realising it she'd started to cry, she was sobbing. Why was Nacho, the only man she'd ever fallen in love with, writing this now, after what he'd done? She pounded her feet and fists on the mattress. The tables can turn, the shark can be preyed upon, the fish can become a shark. We stand alone, we do things and we learn. Knowledge is a journey. We embody an all-knowing consciousness, her grandfather used to say, and then he'd add: in order to exist you must learn to forget. She wasn't herself. Nora and her grandfather had forgotten many things, they'd forgotten everything about their previous lives and the people they had loved, they'd expunged the essential, everything except those people's existence. Her grandfather walked a lot, especially after her mother's death. He covered great distances on foot, always with some acorns in his pocket. He walked nonstop, covering disproportionate, absurd distances to the rattling of his acorns. When Grandmother died it only escalated. In the weeks following his wife's death, Grandfather disposed of so many things. Nora wasn't a walker. She still loved the man, but no matter how hard she tried she couldn't get past the pain he'd caused her. She started nibbling on the letter, biting off pieces and spitting them out. What fell to the floor was nothing other than globs of paper with ink diluted by tears and saliva. She continued until she'd dispensed with the whole letter and the area around her bed looked like a garden at the beginning of a snowstorm.

She knelt on the carpet and started placing the pieces of wet paper, one after the other, in the palm of her hand. Bent over like that, naked, she felt helpless. The mass of paper in her hand prompted a mixture of rage, anguish and desire. She couldn't shake off his scent, his gaze, his skin. Nacho was her, he had been ever since that flight. The mere thought of him filled her with that warm tingle. Great white sharks have a lot in common with serial killers. After they'd all died, Grandfather and Nora had spent years studying sharks. He warned her: never get caught by a shark. Knowing your enemy is the only way to survive. She could rid herself of him, she could walk away if she wanted, but deep down she knew that one way or another, no matter where they both might end up, she would love him; she would not forget, didn't want to forget, that what they had shared was life itself. It would have been absurd to treat it as if it was nothing, because for her it had been so much more than that. It had been the best thing she'd had. An altogether different matter was what to do now. Know your enemy. Who was her enemy? These great predators don't arbitrarily seek out their victims, her grandfather said, they use sophisticated hunting strategies that suggest the calculating minds of bloodthirsty criminals. Don't ever let your guard down! They choose their operational base according to factors such as the number of potential prey and the existence of hiding places from which to catch their victims unawares. Their methods are more successful in environments with little light. Nora thought of the plane, how the lights were dimmed just as they kissed for the first time. She thought, too, of the buxom flight attendant chasing a Coca-Cola can down the aisle, and about the house in Pedralbes. There was something else her grandfather had told her which she'd ignored: the first moments of a relationship are crucial. If you analyse them well you'll be able to interpret everything that follows.

Nora gathered up all the pieces of paper. She closed her fist around them and wept. Still holding them, she tapped her chest a couple of times to help her feel more alive. She got up. And then, standing in front of the toilet, she looked down into the clear, still water in the bowl. One day we'll all be drinking sewer water. She dropped the scraps of paper into the toilet as if sprinkling flour over the mountains in a nativity scene. She watched them float. The ink formed shapes on the paper, dark, thin strips like black streamers: the children in her mind were not at a party but a funeral. She thought about her grandfather and how much he'd walked every day after Grandmother's death, from Sarrià to El Clot, the neighbourhood where he was born, and back again. Sharks continue to hone their hunting skills throughout their lives. Men too! she exclaimed as she flushed the toilet and the bits of paper became a swirl that would soon be gone. Perhaps the letter was sincere, but it was too late. She looked at the spiralling water and took a deep breath, the paper was disappearing fast, they'd reach the sea and fish would eat them. Two scraps remained. She thought of the shark and the sea bream and the kiss they'd shared. Nora hadn't known what kissing was until they met. And that way of his of pinching her nipples, his face when they made love. She stopped crying and climbed back into bed, thinking she'd sleep some more. The wine helped. She downed the rest in one gulp. She saw her phone light up. It was him.

'Hola.'

'Did you get it?'

'I did.'

'And?'

'And nothing.'

'What do you mean? Are you all right, Nora?'

'Since when are you interested in how I am?'

'Please, Nora. I'm so sorry. Please don't leave me!'

'There are some things for which one can't apologise. You don't want me to leave you? What is it that I shouldn't leave? You and I have never been together. You didn't want that.'

Nora had got up and was staring again at the two strips of paper that were still floating in the toilet bowl.

'I love you.'

'You've never loved me.'

'I do now.'

'Too late.'

'I've loved you since the flight, I just couldn't admit it.'

'You're clueless, aren't you?' she yelled as she flushed the toilet again and the two remaining white rectangles were swept away. They were so tiny, the shark and the bream, joined forever.

'I've been through too much, Nora.'

'The letter no longer exists, the toilet ate it, and before that I chewed it to bits. I'll give the roses to the street cleaner. I *did* love you, you know? I did believe in the ashlar stones of the church.'

'You still love me, Nora. I know you do.'

'*Adéu.*'

Nora hung up and pressed the red button until the phone switched off. She lay on the bed with her arms crossed and looked out at the sky. The clouds had dissipated and a plane was flying by, the two white jet trails behind it merging together. She thought again of Christ on the cross. Nacho was gone, it was as easy as pressing the *off* button. The mobile's screen was sweaty. A door had been closed. She was deceiving herself, but that was what she wanted to believe. She hated having sweaty palms. Nacho had taken over her mind and body the day they met, there was nothing else, no one else, and having her mobile off wouldn't change that. It didn't matter that he'd turned her into a whore, the pain didn't matter, or the fact that he loved her now and wanted a life with her. It didn't matter that she continued to fuck his clients. Nothing mattered. Have you ever fallen in love? he'd asked her. Yes, with you.

Sharks can also become prey and be captured, almost always for their fins. In general, humans don't like them, that's why they kill them. So why did she feel safe? Her husband no longer treated her the way he used to, he was getting older, and she had just hung up on the only man she'd ever been in love with. And yet she felt serene. She was afraid of nothing. Grandfather had always made her look good. She lifted a framed photo of him and kissed it. The glass felt cold against her lips. In the picture, her grandfather looked a bit like the white-haired man who waited for his sweetheart every afternoon in front of the local bookstore. She thought about her daughters. What must they be doing now? She'd phone them. When it's cold in the mountains and you have nothing to cover yourself with, the best thing to do is walk. The same is true of life. Grandfather walked a lot, especially after Mother's death.

23

SHE WAS COOKING A THICK CUT OF BEEF. THE SOUND OF sizzling meat is like the sound of rain: thousands of tiny sputtering bubbles. Nora, like her grandfather, didn't use oil, she cut a sliver of fat from the steak and rubbed it over the frying pan. Meat has an uneven texture, the part that is in contact with heat sizzles and crackles, and when you turn it over, it looks like an autumn landscape from a bird's-eye view. She cooked the steak, and thought of the commotion at the market that morning between the butcher and the greengrocer. Have a look! the female butcher exclaimed as she emerged with a suckling pig and plopped it on the counter with its face and legs dangling. Oh lord, it looks like a baby! said the greengrocer, also a woman. To Nora, standing in line to buy meat, the situation symbolised age-old conflicts, most of the wars that had taken place throughout history, even in Westerns. Squabbles between farmers and ranchers. The latter needed large tracts of land to graze their cows. Who were the cowboys? Just that, boys with cows. And farmers needed land to farm. When she gave herself to

Nacho, she was following the dictates of desire, she'd fallen in love for the first time. It hadn't worked out, and he'd made her feel like a piece of raw meat. Not having him, not being with him, was a lot like hell, but Nora had slammed the door shut. It would be difficult, but what in life isn't? Her father and mother, her grandmother, and finally her grandfather as well, were dead, but she'd been the one to kill off what she had with Nacho. For good? Forever? You can't do that overnight, much less in a tangled relationship like theirs. Nacho wouldn't disappear just like that, she knew that much, but in the meantime she would do her own thing.

Survival tools: emotional journeys, spontaneous friendships. She was thinking of *Midnight Cowboy*, about the young Midwesterner who arrives in New York with his guitar and ends up as a sex worker. John Voight. He encounters Dustin Hoffman's character, who tries to help him. They meet, help each other out, become friends. One is tall and wears a brown leather jacket. The other, short and sickly, is always dressed in black. They want to leave New York. They finally scrape together the bus fare and board a Greyhound, then Hoffman dies. Nora had cried as her grandfather held her. She remembered, too, all the times they'd watched *Butch Cassidy and the Sundance Kid*. Two thieves start stealing a bit here and there and eventually turn into proper outlaws. Paul Newman and Robert Redford, handsome, clever, cunning, deceitful. She and her grandfather would watch it together and weep, especially when *Raindrops Keep Fallin' on My Head* played. Those two didn't kill their victims—that part they liked.

Enemies should never be physically killed off. Strength is all in the mind. Nora was surprised to see her grandfather cry. Men don't cry, she'd been told as a child. With Nacho she'd experienced the oldest fear in the book, the fear of rejection, of being undeserving of love or somehow inferior. It's a fear that doesn't arise from the person who feels it, it is passed down from generation to generation.

What must my father have felt? Who can know anything about another person's suffering. In the end, our biggest fear is to be left alone with our pain, to have thought that someone was there for us only to realise that this was not the case. She thought about the Ferris wheel at Tivoli Gardens, the oldest amusement park in the world, in Copenhagen. And about the pirate ship restaurant where she and Robert had dined a couple of times. They still desired each other then. She stared vacantly at the poster they'd brought back from the trip, at the bottom of which was the word *Tivoli* in large letters, the background an electric blue, night blue, and at the top of the poster, a flying white horse. A carousel horse. She'd always wanted to have a horse. And while she thought about Westerns and about suffering, she nervously chewed the blue steak. She was also having an heirloom tomato, and a glass of red wine. Alcohol helped her forget. When you bite into a whole tomato, a burst of cold fills your mouth, and sometimes juice trickles down your hands, chin and neck. She wouldn't be able to work today. Robert had called to say he'd be late. He arrived home later every day, and there were more and more days when he didn't come home at all. It was all the same to Nora. She wondered if the minichefs were still protecting her and her family the way they always had.

She wondered if what was happening was good or bad. If the framed drawing beside the blue cloth, a picture of the four of them drawn by Cloe, had had its moment, completed its life cycle, and was now ready for something else. Everything has its moment. That of the happy family was over, and Nora felt no grief at the loss. No fear. Whatever could be lost had already been lost.

When you wonder if your partner is being unfaithful, it means he's already been unfaithful, so why the need to know more? She headed downstairs to her studio and flopped down on the red sofa, naked. Not being glued to her phone was a relief. She covered herself with the Persian wool blanket. She thought about the time when eating had disgusted her: she'd walk into a restaurant and have to leave because, instead of people having a meal, she saw a bunch of maws swallowing food, fierce ravenous animals that would kill anything in order to survive. It was murderous. Eating was so vulgar. Those maws were killer beasts. She had to do what needed to be done, the problem was she'd forgotten what that was, so she didn't eat, she only slept. She couldn't go without food, but for a while she could only eat if she was alone, without being seen, and she couldn't tolerate the sight of anyone eating. Eating was synonymous with killing, it was a black void, it was murder, it was the end.

She remembered the fishing boats returning to port surrounded by seagulls. She was thinking about Nacho and the shark they had seen as children at the fish market in Palamós. That had never happened. Nacho and she were never together as children, but it could have happened. When it's cold in the mountains and you have nothing to cover yourself with, the best thing to do is walk. The same is true of life. She liked being a high-class hooker. She'd phone the Russian. She couldn't sleep, and her thoughts meandered to corners of her mind that she wasn't in control of. She wanted to continue being a one-night whore; she realised it was what she wanted and that was enough. The Russian had taken over the business in Pedralbes. She would keep going a while longer, until her instincts told her otherwise. She trusted what she felt more than what she heard or thought. She remembered the boy on the skateboard that she'd crossed paths with. He had long curly hair, an expressive face, a strong body; he wore hospital trousers and a short-sleeved T-shirt and was being pulled along by a very large mastiff. There are short spurts of joy, nothing more. The rest is what it is. Those who live to find happiness often kill themselves. Why did her father commit suicide? The sky is an immense poster. What's left when you take it down? The universe. And what is the universe? Another poster. And if you remove that, the universe, what's left? Walls, that's what Jana had told her once when she was a child. What happens to the rest of us when someone we love commits suicide? Where does eternity end, Mamà? Nora fell asleep.

She woke to the sound of rain tapping at the window. For a moment she thought of the meat on the pan, that sizzling sound, and the smell of cooked blood. How good it tasted, she'd eaten it almost raw. She remembered her dream the way someone watches a movie in 3D. She was on her way home. She was walking past the Catholic school when a boy of about eighteen, long curly hair, expressive face and strong body, wearing hospital trousers and a short-sleeved T-shirt, came trundling past on his skateboard, pulled along by a giant dog. They smiled at each other. He stopped and said, Want a ride? Sorry? Hop on and hold tight. Cim will pull us along. Nora had pigtails. She was wearing silver ballet flats, a beret, a black push-up bra and bodice, stockings held up by a garter belt, and a black blazer on top. She hopped on behind the boy and they rode down the street without stopping until they reached the roundabout. She held onto him and imagined he was Nacho. They'd ridden like that thirty years before when they went from La Fosca to Palamós. The dog pulled hard and everything whizzed by. Nora's breasts were glued to the boy's back. She could feel her heartbeat and how hard her nipples were. He stopped at the roundabout, beside a campervan with no wheels that was parked in the middle. It looked familiar. Night had fallen, a sign lit up. RAINBOW. The letters were like the ones she'd drawn on ruled paper when she was a child. The boy had stopped his skateboard because a car was passing. Nora thanked him. You're not going any further? No. Why? I don't need to. I like you. You could be my son. But I'm not. Nora petted the dog for a moment, then she said goodbye and left. *Dancin' Clown* was still playing when the boy disappeared down Balmes. Nora turned and walked up the avenue, a gold ball in each hand. She hadn't asked him his name.

She was still lying on the red sofa. Her grandfather was a man who needed to say what he thought so that he could continue to believe the things he said. Without Nacho life was as grey as before. Nora remembered when Jana was five and her friend Maria Pou confessed that she was in love with Nil. And who is this Nil, Maria? A boy in your class? No, he's a fifteen-year-old on my brother's football team and he's really handsome. Can I tell you a secret? I wrote him a letter. And what did the letter say? Nil, please don't forget me, even if I'm bad. As long as boys love girls everything will be fine! Maria Pou exclaimed. Nora was letting all sorts of things pop into her head to avoid doing what she wanted to do. Enough indecision. She preferred Paul Newman to Robert Redford.

'Yuri?' She'd dialled the number, it hadn't been so difficult after all.

'Speaking. Who's calling?'

The Russian spoke perfect Catalan, though his consonants were a little strong, especially his r's. She liked his tone of voice, the calm it conveyed.

'It's Nora. I have a proposal.'

'Hola Nora. I've heard good things about you. The painter!'

'*Gràcies.*'

'By the way, did you know the Chinese are planning to send a twelfth astronaut on their journey to Mars?'

'Sorry?'

'She'll be a space whore. Like they used to do on long-haul ships until the nineteenth century: there was always a catamite, a *maricón* that everyone fucked and who almost never made it to port.'

The Russian had pronounced the word *maricón* exactly like her grandfather did, stressing the consonants more than necessary.

'What was that again?'

'Nothing, just that two-by-three metre cubicles are becoming popular in Russia. They're like public lavatories, but with a bed. And anyone can go in and do whatever they want. I'm thinking of starting a business like that here.'

'Ah, yes,' said Nora. 'I'm not interested.'

'Of course not. You're of a different ilk, another class of woman. I was just toying with the idea when you rang.'

'Right.'

'Never set foot in Russia ...'

'Wasn't planning to.'

'Good. It's my country, but ... so why are you calling?'

'I'd like us to do business together.'

'Is this about your paintings?'

'My paintings?' The man was full of surprises.

'I like your work.'

'Actually, I was calling because I wanted to continue working as an escort. But only with certain customers, a few, well-chosen ones that I could vet ... We could go fifty-fifty.' She spat it out nervously, but the way he spoke had a soothing effect. Nothing fazed the guy, it was all the same to him, whether he was talking about astronaut number twelve, paintings, or whoring.

'Well, I've already told you I'm interested in your work.'

'Gràcies.'

'When do you want to start?'

'When you have someone specific in mind.'

'I've got one right now. A woman who used to work as a life model. Well-read, has money. She wants to come to the house. She's never been with a woman and wants to try. Have you been with a woman?'

'No.'

'Shall I notify you of the day and time?'

'Yes.'

Phoning the Russian hadn't been as difficult as she'd thought it would be. Nora sat at the piano. She wanted to start a new painting, one with a woman in it. Nora didn't know what she believed in anymore. Be yourself! her grandfather had said. She was trying. She thought of Júlia. Why had she never done it with her? One of Robert's fantasies was to watch two women having sex, that's why he liked being in their company. Júlia and Nora would touch each other and he would watch. Keep going, live. She was staring blankly at the poster again, at that white horse she imagined powerful. Tivoli Gardens, the oldest amusement park in the world.

24

WHAT THE RUSSIAN MAN DIDN'T SAY WAS THAT IT WAS A BLACK girl, young and thin, with huge breasts and silver rings in her nipples. Her best customer yet would turn out to be a woman. Nora had dressed like in the dream with the young skate-boarder, but instead of ballet flats she was wearing black patent boots with stiletto heels that came up to her knees. Again she imagined she was watering the plants. It can be an important job. Watering is like praying with water.

'Do you know why there are no fisherwomen?' Nora asked the girl.

'No clue.'

While her customer responded, Nora dropped her coat on the floor, revealing her rhinestone encrusted bra, bodice, garter belt, stockings ... The girl's eyes widened when she saw that Nora wasn't wearing knickers and had shaved her pubic hair, making her look like a doll. She caressed Nora between the legs. I like you. She had on a black strapless dress and stiletto heels. She was taller than Nora and much thinner. I love your full breasts, your belly! she said.

'I'd like to be a fisherwoman.'

The girl laughed at the comment and bit Nora's lip for a moment. She had a wide, warm tongue.

'My name's Maria,' she said. 'You know why I'm here?'

'No... I'm Nora.'

She didn't know why she'd given her real name, she never did that with customers, but she felt differently about this woman. She felt she could trust her. She suddenly realised that she rarely asked any questions and knew very little about any of the things that truly mattered; she'd always needed someone else to point out their value. She painted out of necessity, but she wasn't always aware of what it was she was painting. Robert had been a counterbalance, the external gaze that made her see the importance of certain things. But her husband had been gone too long, and now she sailed alone and watered the plants.

'I've gone off men,' Maria said. 'The ones I don't fancy want to fuck me.' She was licking Nora's face. 'And the ones I do fancy fall in love with me but can't fuck me.'

'Why not?'

That was all Nora could say before Maria started kissing her again. She had a special way of teasing her mouth; she would brush her tongue over her lips, dip inside her mouth, then move back to her face, and as she did this she gently caressed her breasts, barely touching them. Then she pinched her nipple until it hurt. Nora liked it. Then she caressed her again. You're so pretty. There's a special strength about you, a liquid coldness ... something. I just don't get men. She continued to talk as she caressed Nora. She discovered that if she inserted her finger into Nora's anus and withdrew it quickly, Nora trembled. It was the physical experience of loss. Nora's body reacted by shaking, and she moaned. Maria penetrated her again with her finger and then hugged her. Nora lay on the bed, legs parted, arms crossed, and let herself go. She arched her back when Maria fingered her yet again. Nora embraced her, and as Maria covered her face and neck with little kisses, Nora tugged at the silver nipple rings, afraid to hurt her, though she told her it didn't hurt, to pull harder. They lay together on a round bed with a ceiling mirror above it. Maria's hand contrasted with Nora's paler skin, and this excited her. It was a novel experience. Today I hung out two loads of clothes, Maria said, with my son sitting on the floor beside me. He was looking at me and I asked him, What do you do when you like someone and they like you too, but the person doesn't want to play with you? That never happens! he said. Why? Because if we like each other we play together. Yes, but imagine if it did happen. I'd kill him! my son said with a laugh, assuming a karate stance. Then he looked me in the eye and said, I don't know what I'd do.

'Your son's right.'

The girl touched her like no man ever had, she had a different rhythm. Maria didn't penetrate her, she just ran her finger, her hand, around her sex, her bum, and bit her nipples. Nora inhaled her scent. She was discovering that she liked doing it with a woman. Maria continued to suck on her lips and lick her face. And then Nora heard a familiar-sounding moan coming from the next room.

'I know he is,' Maria said, 'but this has happened to me five times in the last six years and I'm starting to think it's me. I fall for married men. I'm married myself, but that has nothing to do with it. I love my husband. They fall in love right back and they tell me so. But then they say they can't fuck me, that they're either with their wives or they're with me. I don't get it. I don't want them to leave their wives. I'm fine as I am. I just want what should happen to happen.'

She finished her sentence and revealed her nakedness to Nora. She hadn't been wearing anything under her dress and there she lay with her silver rings, her full bush. Nora thought for a moment about the familiar moaning, but she couldn't hear anything now. She started licking Maria.

'Can I share my love story with you?' Maria said, smiling and furrowing her brows. Nora was underneath her looking up. The woman had a special way of raising her eyebrows when smiling, forming a hillock covered with dark snow. 'I was on a school field trip to Isla Fantasía when I realised I was feeling a sort of love I might never experience again. I was in one of the pools when I suddenly understood I was falling in love at the very moment that it was happening.'

Nora kept licking and listened to Maria's prattle. Isla Fantasía! That waterpark with slides and such ... but strangely Nora was riveted, she found it more interesting than most anything else she might be told. 'We were thirteen years old and my classmates were flinging themselves down the slides left and right. A boy named Manel had been sliding with me, we hugged on the way down and continued to hold each other after we'd coasted into the pool. The slide ended in a very large pool, and he hugged me from behind as we stood there without speaking, in that massive pool, gazing up at the sky. I could feel his breath on my neck, his whole body against mine. Our backs were burning in the sun, but that was all right. I watched four planes go by, they moved across the sky and disappeared. I felt that the sky was small and the pool infinite. I've never been back to Isla Fantasía. I worry that I can no longer feel that kind love. What are *you* afraid of?'

Just as Maria posed the question, Nora jumped up.

'What's wrong?'

They were at the house in Pedralbes, where she went on that first night with Nacho, a place Nora knew well. She'd been there twenty-four times, with different men. She'd counted them. Then she'd painted them. One night only. And now with a woman. She knew all its secrets, knew that voyeurs abounded and there were peepholes in every room. The spyhole in their room was behind a painting of a red-tailed mermaid half-submerged in water. The waves were blue glitter, the mermaid's torso rose out of the sea. Her wispy waist made her large breasts seem bigger; with her right hand she cupped them, and she raised her left hand skyward, her fingers holding a diamond, as if imploring to some unknown God, or perhaps abandoning herself to passion. The entire frame was covered with gold glitter. The mermaid's lips were red like her tail, and her straight brown hair cascaded down her back into the water. The mermaid wasn't pretty, she was sexy, with huge black eyes and long eyelashes. Nora realised that Nacho had been her mentor, he'd taught her how to abandon herself to passion. With him she'd surrendered as never before, and now she could give herself in the same way whenever she wanted. She, who had always identified with control and restraint, was discovering the pleasure of letting go, even when it entailed danger. For some time now, Nora had been prepared to risk it *all*. She'd finally understood that what she had thought of as all wasn't real.

Help me move this painting. Of course! Together they peeped through the hole: on the other side, a man in his fifties was struggling to hold his own with an imposing prostitute who resembled the siren in the painting: the same breasts and red lips. Watching them turned her on, Maria said, and suddenly Nora had a strange fit of laughter. Maria looked at her expectantly. Nora's laugh conveyed sorrow.

'It's so hot in here. Don't you think it's hot, Maria? I feel like a tadpole in the middle of an enormous bathtub filled with hot water. I'm swimming through the tub. I'm drowning. Those two are really going at it aren't they?'

'Yes, he can't keep up with her though. But he has something about him that I like.'

'That's my husband.'

Nora laughed hysterically as Maria stared at her. Then Maria's arms wrapped around her and tried to pull her away from the peephole where Nora stood frozen. She wanted to get Nora back on the bed, but her body wouldn't move, it was rock solid. Nora didn't shed a tear, she didn't scream. She had a blank look on her face. The only thing she felt was that strange heat. She was a tadpole floating in hot water and at the same time she was an outside observer to the scene between her husband and the prostitute, refracted through her own naked body, a woman's body, glued to the peephole, breathing, watching. The prostitute had light skin, long curly black hair, and buck teeth. She looked a bit like a horse, there was something masculine about her. She took her husband's cock in her mouth and told him she wanted to drink his milk, and he liked it. He pushed the girl's head down until she couldn't breathe. It was so hot. The bathtub water was boiling, all Nora could think about was the tadpole. Robert, Saint Robert ... His law firm was failing, he'd been sacking people every day. Things weren't going well. He didn't know how he'd manage. All those times he'd simply disappeared, the trips. Saint Robert, the most faithful man on Earth ... Nora was the tadpole woman now, and Robert had his own secret. So much travelling! The most faithful man on Earth doesn't exist, Júlia always said. What was that? Nora asked. Maria had got Nora on the bed, she had stretched her out on her back and put her head between Nora's legs. Now she was giving her a neck massage. Every now and then she stopped to kiss her face. Some things one should never have to see.

'... empty your mind, just let go. Don't think. Don't worry. Your husband is in the next room and you're here. He doesn't know you're here, does he?'

'No.'

'And you didn't know he was in there.'

'No.'

'Well, now you know. So what? You're the same as you were ten minutes ago. We're still us, regardless of what the people we love do.'

'I thought he'd always been faithful. I thought there was no other woman for him but me ... '

'And that's probably true. For men, seeing prostitutes doesn't count as being unfaithful. So why are you an escort?'

'I don't know. I've been running away from things for such a long time.'

The way Maria was touching her was helping Nora relax. There was a tightness in her chest, but with Maria's massaging, she was beginning to breathe better.

'What are you running from?'

'Myself.'

'I'd love to see you in a Catholic school uniform.'

'Really? You're strange, Maria. I think I like you.'

'I like you too.'

They talked, and Maria continued massaging Nora. Robert with a whore! She wouldn't mention it. What should she say? Why shouldn't she forgive? Adultery was forgivable. Of course it was! After more than twenty years of marriage and two daughters, how could she not understand that he'd want to fuck others and do it dirty. And why not? She liked it too. What she felt at that moment was something else altogether. She was pissed off. Adultery is forgivable, so is whoring. The problem is how to manage anger, the fear of loss, the feeling of having been betrayed. Deceived. Betrayal is cultural, she thought. But she hadn't been afraid of anything for a long time, or so she believed. She was still overheated, the tadpole floating through space, but she knew it would pass. On the other hand, she'd just thought of a way to give Robert a surprise.

She remembered the tree stumps in front of the beach apartment, her finger inside the rotten wood, the worm, the slime. Sure you're not late? the man had asked her. Yes, I'm sure. She walked out onto the terrace where she'd been the first night, to breathe. The clouds were in the shape of a map. Tasmania. Maybe she should go there. Her eyes glanced around in all directions, darting from left to right. She didn't know where to fix her gaze. She looked up at the sky again. She would have liked to live among the clouds, coming together and then dissolving every day. The faces of her customers flashed through her mind, blending into a kaleidoscope. A year of different faces and bodies. She ambled around the terrace like a trapped mouse, thinking all the while, and she started to see what was happening around her. She felt the void left by Nacho and realised that their bond was stronger than she'd imagined. She thought again about the Russian. She remembered Joyce Pensato, the visual artist from New York. The winter she and Nacho had spent together had been the warmest of her life.

25

ROBERT AWOKE WITH ONE THING ON HIS MIND: TO CREATE A microclimate in the greenhouse and import wasps to pollinate his tropical figs. Nora, however, was thinking about seaport protocols and what she'd witnessed the day before: Robert doing it with that whore while she was with Maria. The ship leaves port. Ships always end up leaving port. In the background, the radio. And Nacho phoning nonstop. She hadn't answered his calls in over a week. He left her messages asking her to run away with him. They'd be lovers holding hands. He said he was afraid of the dark but the fear vanished when he was with her. They both had a secret, it showed in their eyes, and yes, when he dived underwater he feared being caught like a fish, he'd always had that fear, but on the day he'd first posed his question—have you ever been in love—he'd been too ashamed to admit it. Too afraid to love. Not anymore. He read stories to her, left them on her voicemail. I'm scared you won't answer me, and without you there's nothing. Nora had decided to leave him, she'd tell him the next time she saw him. She needed to face the world alone. She'd make him wait, so his hands would sweat like hers had. Not that she didn't love him, but now she needed to stop.

... unlike the necessary relationships that exist in nature, plant-pollinator relationships are almost always optional and quite flexible: the disappearance of a pollinator or plant doesn't necessarily mean the extinction of the other partici-pant in the interaction, as alternatives are available to each of them: animals may find other sources of food, and plants other species of pollinators. Robert read aloud to her in bed.

'I'm busy with Kawakami.' Nora was reading *Surrender to Passion* and thinking about Nacho and that short story by Hemingway. But the only one sharing her bed was her husband, who the previous evening had been fucking a whore and was now going on about pollination. Sure, they had alternatives. All the alternatives in the world. And there was always the option of not depending on anything or any-one. We're all strange, but Robert was a little less of a mystery now. She could still see him fucking his whore and moaning like he'd never done with her. It hurt. But the pain was for them both: they had never had that kind of sex.

'Right,' said Robert, who was engrossed in his manual and hadn't heard her.

'Want me to read to you?' Nora was making an effort. When you have to make an effort it means that love is gone. She wanted to be free like oranges and lemons, which don't spoil if they don't come into contact with each other.

What the hell was she doing? She didn't want to touch anyone who reminded her of him; more than ever she wanted to be free. At least Robert wasn't that good anymore. Was that what *The Blue Angel* was about? The fall from a principled, moral life into a pit of your own making. Nora had emerged as the saviour of all that is stifled by our day-to-day existence. What *was* she doing? Living, letting go. From the outside, people would think she'd gone mad, she was closing doors behind her, but they were doors she never should have opened. Lying there in bed she felt as if she were floating on her back.

'Did you say something?' Robert asked, still immersed in his pollination handbook and thinking of tropical figs.

'I said would you like me to read you some Kawakami?'

'No, thanks. I'm heading over to the greenhouse.'

Nora closed her eyes and imagined herself making love with Nacho. She could feel it. Now that she'd decided it was over with him, she was repulsed by Robert. She didn't want him to touch her. Her interest in Robert had been rekindled while Nacho existed, but now it was all coming to an end. And it wasn't about the prostitute, that part she found natural enough. At least she'd discovered that her husband wasn't completely dead. She thought again about port protocols. A lover in every port. Fig pollination, that was pure Robert: from flower to flower, but always the same flower at home, if at all possible an artificial one. It was better than having to water it every day. It was like her grandfather's vase. Real flowers are too much work. Nora had become Robert's perfect artificial flower. At home. And each with their own life. A port is a place intended for the flow of goods, people and information, or to receive and provide security to the boats and ships responsible for them. She thought of the Countess of Segovia who had died because a man had sworn his undying love for her. She didn't want to stay with Robert or for Robert to stay with her because he owed it to her. The fragility of it all! What had been Nacho's role in her life? Who was Robert? Are you sure you're not running late? the rabbit cabbie would have exclaimed. For some time now Nora had started to see things more clearly: she'd realised that nothing is ever what it appears to be. She'd learned that only by loving all people can you survive great heartbreak. She would do just that from now on. More customers. More faces. More bodies. More paintings. And, yes, she did have a secret. She wanted to talk to Robert. She went to look for him in the greenhouse and found him sitting on the floor looking up at the tropical figs.

'All any of us know of love comes from just a few people, the love of certain people. The faces of the people I've loved have been with me all my life; yours, the girl's, Grandfather's. What about you?' She sat down in front of him as she said this. Their toes were touching. Robert looked at her.

'Sorry—what?'

'Who could love all people at the same time?'

'What are you talking about? One of those books you're reading? ... I've got work to do, and we should go to Habitat. What's the plan?'

'A whore, that's who.'

'What?' Robert glanced at the figs again, wondering what was going on with his wife. 'What's got into you? All these shows you've been doing, it's starting to take its toll.' Had she had someone spy on him?

'Nothing. I'm fine ... .'

They sat there silently, looking into each other's eyes. They hadn't looked at each other like that for a long time. It was making him nervous.

'I don't want you to be with me out of obligation, Robert. I don't want you to stay with me because you feel like you owe it to me.'

'What are you talking about?'

'Promise me you wouldn't do that.'

'I'm with you because I love you. I've always loved you.'

'Shall we say, six, then?' Nora said on her way out of the greenhouse.

'Sure, but aren't you going to paint today?' His question went unanswered, she was gone. Robert felt miserable, lonely. They hadn't made love for days.

Life, her life, would never be the same, it was what it was, and hers was changing fast. The seagulls were gaining ground, they were pinching children's sandwiches. Watering the plants was a form of prayer. Robert watered often, and so did she.

26

THEY HAD AGREED TO MEET AT A BAR INSIDE THE TUBE station at Plaça Catalunya. Nacho would have preferred the oyster bar. He was already there when Nora arrived, and she studied him from a distance. He'd told her that he hadn't slept for four days. She missed her piece of rubber. She gave him a quick peck on the cheek, turning her head away. He was sitting on a barstool. There was enough noise and anonymity there to do what needed to be done and then go their separate ways, as if that plane had never even taken off.

'Hola,' she said simply.

'Hola,' he replied, and launched into his spiel. 'I know you want to dump me, Nora. I know you're hurt, plain and simple. Since my mother died I've never loved a woman, or anyone else, without feeling the need to clip their wings, never until now have I loved without judging, never loved anyone I couldn't subdue, and yet with you I don't even want to try. I did what I did. I fucked up. I know it, and I'm sorry. I don't want anything from anyone. I just want you.'

Nora stared at a piece of chewing gum that was stuck to the floor, a large, grimy piece of gum that the soles of many shoes had trodden on. *The sole of a shoe isn't the sole part of it, it's attached to the shoe.* For years that was what Júlia had on her answering machine. She wondered if Nacho's speech was prepared or if it was spontaneous.

'... I need you to be yourself. I don't just love you, I believe what you say. I believe you, and believing you helps me grow as a person. Things are happening to me that I've never experienced before, and I've come to realise that I hold you above everything and everyone, above time and space, I just do.'

For some reason, Nora saw in the chewing gum that had been trodden on a thousand times, the boar's head that her grandfather had kept in the dining room of the farmhouse in Bordils. She'd always been afraid of it, though she never told her grandfather. Maybe things would have gone better for them if they'd talked about their fears, but they'd watched shark documentaries instead.

'It's too late. Spare me the speech, the bullshit. Did you memorise all that? I just came to say goodbye.' It was no longer gum, but that boar with its red tongue hanging out.

'I don't believe you. You love me as much as I love you. Nora, you've changed me. Couldn't we go somewhere else?'

She shook her head.

'I need a drink', he said.

'I'll just have water.'

'Champagne, please. The best you have.'

The guy behind the bar gave Nacho a look that said *where the hell does this idiot think he is?*

'Your best champagne. That should be clear enough, no?'

The barman looked like he wanted to spit in Nacho's face, but instead he ignored him.

'I just want water,' Nora said again, still seeing the chewing-gum boar. She wasn't looking at Nacho or the man behind the bar or anyone else. Today she had only one goal.

'Actually, make it a Krug.'

'A what?' The barman was fed up with this posh couple who had decided to brave the tube station bar.

Nora stared intently at the gum. Nacho was starting to lose his temper. She thought of the flying white horse on the Tivoli Gardens poster.

'*El más caro que tenga, señor,*' Nacho said.

The waiter placed a piccolo-bottle of Codorniu in front of him. It was warm. He served it in two plastic cups.

'Shall we toast?'

Nora stared at the gum without reacting. Nacho toasted her cup and took a sip of the undrinkable lukewarm cava, then continued as if nothing had happened.

'After Mother's death, I was like a wall where people's words collided. I refused to learn, to share, to allow anyone to decide anything for me. Now I'm finally capable of feeling. A barrier has come down, I'm not sure why, but it's gone.'

Nora wasn't listening.

'I know I'm a bit strange, but I've matured more since that London flight than in the last thirty years. I'd locked myself away in a dark room and now I'm emerging. Please forgive me, Nora. I know I've let you down.'

'You disappointed me once,' Nora said, impulsively raising her head.

She had shifted her attention from the chewing gum to one of those combo meals that sit behind the bar all day: a yellowing sausage and some French fries that looked more rubbery than the chewing gum on the floor, and ketchup that was veering towards a shade somewhere between orange and brown. She remembered the day Cloe had asked, Mamà, are those French fries made of potatoes? She looked at the cold food and then at him. She wasn't listening. She didn't move. It was the perfect place to say goodbye.

'I'll never let you down again.' He ordered two bottles of cold water.

'You can't disappoint me because I no longer expect anything from you. I believed in you. But it's too late now. You're a fake and you always have been, just like these plastic wine glasses. You asked me once if I'd ever been in love. Yes, with you!'

He tried to hug her and she pushed him away.

'Don't touch me!'

'If you don't want me, I'll cease to exist.'

Nora wasn't even looking at him.

'I told you once, I'm possessive, controlling, manipulative. I judge others as harshly as I do myself. I always keep score, I take more than I give ... none of that works with you.'

Silence. He was staring at her. Her eyes were fixed on the dried-up sausage. She had a sip of water and took a deep breath. Nacho needed Nora to say something, but she didn't take the bait. A disgusting boar. She concentrated on that image, on that alone ... then she began to speak.

'My father killed himself. And do you think I cried? No. I was a little girl and he was a weakling. Nacho, you're a fake and nothing you can do will ever change that.'

For a moment he thought that things were taking a turn for the better.

'If I had never met you I could've gone on with my life,' he said.

'… and my mother's heart broke, it was love and emptiness that did it, the emptiness that comes after losing one's true love. Do you know anything about true love?' she asked with that liquid coldness of hers.

'Yes, Nora, I do. My mother's love, and yours.'

'Right.'

'I never expected, at thirty-five, to feel anything new. With you it was as if a whole new world of knowledge opened up to me, through pleasure. I know you'll find it hard to believe, but I've never been much into kissing, and I don't remember ever looking at a woman and being mesmerised. You've returned me to the person I was before my mother died. She used to weep just looking at landscapes.'

Nora was unmoved. You have to anticipate the enemy's moves to avoid being wounded. She continued:

'Grandmother ended up broken-hearted too, and I was left with my grandfather, there was no one else. And then Robert. You don't exist, Nacho. This is the last time we'll see each other. You're a phoney!'

'You can't turn off love just like that. You need me as much as I need you. I don't believe you. Nora, please forgive me. I want to be with you!'

'There's nothing to believe.'

She focused her mind on the revolting wild boar and the vacant look in her grandmother's eyes after her daughter died. Grandmother abandoned them too. Why? Nora was just a little girl. Why didn't they think of her?

'With you I finally feel secure,' he said. 'I can drop my mask, and suddenly some of the things that filled me with darkness and despair seem silly. I understand things now that I couldn't or didn't want to before, and some other important things, like what we have together, I don't need to understand, I just need to live them. I've stripped naked, done away with shitloads of baggage that I'd accumulated over the years and dressed in clothes that fit me like a glove, something I never expected to have. I don't believe you when you say you don't feel anything. I don't believe you, Nora. It's a way of protecting yourself. I know I hurt you, and I'm asking you to forgive me. I will make it up to you. I love you.'

'It all sounds like a lie, and you are the biggest lie of all. There's no making amends for pain!'

She looked down at the chewing gum: the wild boar was chain smoking, someone had stuffed a cigarette in its mouth. The wild boar and the yellow sausage—in that moment little else seemed to exist. And the din of the bar. Every now and then the train rumbled past, the floor vibrated. The underground bar was the perfect place for an ending.

'I'm done with your speeches, Nacho. I've had enough of your words, which are just that, words. Don't phone me or write to me. *Adéu.* I am the one who's a survivor.'

'*Bueno, thank god it's over, she's gone and left the wanker,*' said the server in Spanish to an old man seated at the bar.

'Don't leave me.'

She climbed the stairs and was outside. She wasn't heading in any particular direction. In the middle of the square a seagull stopped at her feet and stared up at her. She thought of Nacho. She'd just left him, she'd said goodbye. So what? They were so different that someday, someone, somewhere, might mistake one for the other. She looked up at the sky. She strolled along, thinking, not really noticing anything; she was having trouble breathing and stroked her chest with her left hand. She reached inside her pocket but didn't find any acorns. Without realising it, she walked from Plaça Catalunya all the way home. The lights were off. It was growing dark. At times she was filled with intense self-hatred. She caught a scent of lavender. Robert had planted a whole meadow of it and now the scent seemed to rain down from the sky. She remembered the story of the couple who became immortal after they committed adultery and were condemned to live together forever. They should never have gone near each other, but they met secretly. After five hundred years, they probably knew everything there was to know; he'd been a school bus driver for sixty of them, she'd worked the box office at the same cinema since the beginning of the previous century …. Nora suddenly realised that she'd been with Nacho for more than a year. It was hard to imagine life without him. The cold air caressed her nose, her forehead. A small elephant fell on top of me once. It didn't hurt me though.

27

LIE TO ME. TELL ME ALL THESE YEARS YOU'VE WAITED. SHE read this sentence while painting a new canvas. Her mobile was locked away in a drawer. She grew bored when she wasn't having sex with him; she could do it with others, but without him her life had lost its meaning. She'd asked him once: why do you hurt me? Because I enjoy it. She'd closed her eyes and he'd taken her face in both hands and said: Look at me! Nora did, and she saw a strong man. Then she closed her eyes again. Pain relaxed her. The new painting was of Nacho and Maria.

For a lover who has left a relationship but remains in love, the hours take on a character unrelated to the passage of time. The fear of losing the other is the fear of losing oneself. Nora painted. Not having him, not being with him, was too much like hell. She removed her smock and began to dress. She was meeting Yuri in a bar downtown, she wanted to see him in person. She decided to walk there. She was wearing gladiator's sandals and a black strappy dress that caught between her legs as she moved. It's useless to deny love when it touches you personally. When you break off a relationship, you're attempting to win a battle against time. You start over and reset the timer, or at least that's the initial feeling you have. Monotony is a killer. It was May, the feeling of summer was in the air. Nora walked on seemingly unburdened, breathing calmly. Her dress rubbed against her naked body. When she arrived at the bar she saw that the metal tables had been moved outside. From the corner she spotted the Russian sitting alone. Nacho had said that he looked like Paul Newman. He recognised her too. He was waiting for her with his legs crossed, a calm look on his face. He was wearing red shoes and had white hair; his blue eyes stared at her.

'Hola. This is one of my favourite bars.'

Nora nodded as they kissed each other on the cheek and she sat down without responding.

'So, you want to be the one to choose,' the Russian Newman said, not beating around the bush. 'That's fine with me.'

'I came so I could put a face to the name.'

'I already had a face for yours, you're the painter of the moment.'

Nora smiled. She hated flattery. 'Thanks.'

'You know I like your paintings, I have some of them at home ... Fine by me. My clients are loyal, so I'm able to provide their age and background for you to choose. A painter of your calibre can't go with just anyone.'

Again she noticed the man's almost-perfect Catalan, and his strong hands, which gestured as he spoke. Whenever he finished a long sentence he closed his eyes.

'I'll want a full report then.'

'You'll have it, not a problem, we drew one up for the life model. I'm keen on having you work for me, so of course I want you to be happy ... by the way, I mentioned multifunctional systems the other day, didn't I? What's your take on that?'

'You did, yes, but I'm afraid I wasn't paying enough attention', Nora said.

Yuri was cutting pieces of dry sausage as they talked. What was the man doing slicing fuet while seated at an outdoor café? And why was he cutting such thick pieces? It was a sunny day. They both put on their sunglasses at the same time. Nora's were a pair of large Paul Frank shades she'd had for years, the Russian's were horn-rimmed, round and small in a Beatles kind of style. They looked good on him. Nora ordered a shandy. Under the table, her gladiator's sandals were very close to his red shoes. In fact, her almost bare feet rested between those crimson extremities that tapped rhythmically while the man blathered on about multifunctional systems. Nora took a deep breath and smiled. She didn't smile often.

'... Researchers are trying to do the same thing now, applying self-assembly to macro architecture. If they succeed, it would allow what I was telling you about the other day, about multifunctional systems.'

Yuri continued speaking, and this time Nora was aware that she was listening to him. She and Nacho had sat at this outdoor cafe once, more than a year ago. Sometimes she closed her eyes and could still feel him. The Russian reeled off stories that seemed meaningless, but he managed to make them interesting.

'Yes, multifunctional systems ... I remember that,' Nora said, satisfied with herself because she was following the conversation.

'But you agree with me, right? A world with a different product for every need has brought us to the mess we're in today. It has to change.' Yuri respected anyone who could get fired up and see projects through to fruition.

'Maybe you're right.' When she didn't know what to say, she always agreed with the other person.

'In the long run, what we need is a single system that allows us to do all kinds of things.'

'That would be good.'

They were both silent. Yuri looked at her and exhaled. Nora was nibbling on a slice of *fuet*. Her mind drifted to the story her grandfather had told her as a child: before they built the road to the remote village, loneliness made the women hurl themselves into the sea. The dry sausage was good. Nora, where are you? The man had come to know her better in that short space of time than others had over the course of a lifetime. You remind me of my grandfather. You look sad. Yes, but that has nothing to do with my grandfather ... I'll be off then, it was nice meeting you; you can tell me about it another day, when we have more time, I like listening to you. She started walking, still breathing in the scent of the Russian. The clouds had formed a map in the sky. It was Tasmania.

28

WHEN THE CHILD WAS A CHILD, IT DIDN'T KNOW THAT IT WAS a child. Wim Wenders. *Wings of Desire.* The opening had been another resounding success, and Nora glanced around the near-empty gallery. She was wearing a short vintage dress with black and white embroidery, knee-high black boots and the Sgt Pepper's jacket that Nacho had given her. She liked the gold buttons. She'd seen him earlier in the evening and had greeted him coldly, then lost track of him in the crowd. Now that the event was ending and almost everyone had left, she spotted him staring at her from a corner of the room. He looked haggard. Robert hadn't even put in an appearance. At least now she knew it wasn't because he was working. She closed her eyes and recalled her grandfather's words. Be yourself! At first she hadn't noticed that Nacho was walking towards her. She looked at him. How could I know anything other than myself? They kissed on the cheek, and she turned her head to avoid his lips. What she really wanted was to make love to him right there on the gallery floor.

'When I was a kid I had a toy figure with a Sgt Pepper's jacket like that. A little tin soldier. I cried when I lost him. Mother said, Don't worry, you'll find him again one day. It looks good on you.'

'Hola, Nacho, how are you?'

'I'm not sure.' He was fiddling with something in his left pocket.

'You're that little soldier.'

'You were right. I miss you.'

'Me too, even now.'

'Yeah ... .'

It had been several months since they'd last spoken. She'd had a few other customers apart from Maria, but seeing him still filled her with that familiar warmth.

'I had lunch with my father.'

'Oh?'

'My real father! The man who was there that day, who saw my dead mother's blue face. The man I thought had killed my mother, turns out he's my father. Can you guess who he is? ... you know him.'

'I think so, yes.'

Nora thought about Tatami Man, and what he'd said. It was the first time she'd worked as a prostitute. *Every now and then I feel like having sex. Or rather, I feel like being with a woman who isn't my wife. Like today. So I shower, put on nice clothes, my best cologne, and I do exactly that ... don't turn around! And then I calm down for a few days. I hope you're enjoying this.* The man's hands in the car, on the gear shift, and the yellow balloon tied to the boy's wrist. *I'm going to cover your eyes and face with a blue cloth ... I've*

*never been able to do it again with anyone whose face isn't
covered with a blue cloth. You remind me of her.*

'Nora, are you listening?'

Nora hadn't heard a thing Nacho had said, she was still
lost in that first winter afternoon, with the man who'd fucked
her from behind, her own mixture of tenderness and detach-
ment, and the realisation that she'd enjoyed it.

'Nora, did you hear me?' Nacho said again. 'I'm telling
you that you did it with my father, all for a game that I cooked
up. I'm disgusted with myself.' He couldn't even look at her.

'Nacho, don't be, it's not worth it. Disgusted about what?'

He was still looking at his shoes and fumbling with something in his pocket. He was trembling.

'I don't know what will happen, but I don't hate you anymore. Thanks to you I discovered a Nora who had been too
afraid to live. I need time ... one day you'll realise you're
living a life that isn't your own. That's what you told me. And
you were right.'

'Nora, you fucked my father.'

'I did it with my grandfather, too.'

Nacho finally raised his head. Nora realised she'd revealed
what she'd never told anyone. Her deepest secret. Now she
was the one looking down and shaking all over. She started
to sob uncontrollably and dropped to the floor, leaning against
the wall. She sat with her legs folded, hunched over, hugging
her knees. Nacho embraced her. He started to kiss her.

'Don't touch me. Just leave! I'm the one who has reasons
to be disgusted with myself', she cried.

'There's no reason to feel that way. Nora, I miss you ter-
ribly. If you stop breathing, the whole world stops turning.'

He reluctantly strode out of the room, dragging his feet. Nora didn't respond or look up to watch him go, too repulsed by what she'd done. She sat there curled up, surrounded by paintings with red dots. Once again she'd sold everything on opening night. Grandfather would have been proud. I sense you're hiding something, a deep pain, an enigma. She could hear his voice. You, too, are a survivor. I know. I can tell. She'd never told anyone. She remembered seeing herself reflected in Nacho's eyes, the face of a woman who appeared serene but was hiding something, a big secret. What had happened? She'd promised her grandfather never to speak of it. She had promised. She was still crying, but now it was a calm weeping. A voice interrupted her. Nora, I'm so sorry, but is there anything else I should do? It was the intern at the gallery. He reminded her of the boy in her dream who was skateboarding down Tibidabo Avenue with his dog Cim. No, thanks, that's it ... well, actually, just one more thing. Would you mind sitting here and holding me?

What were amusement parks really? Places people went in order not to think.

29

THE EASIEST DAY WAS YESTERDAY. NORA HAD ARRIVED AT THE house in Pedralbes hours ago. She wanted to avoid any slip-ups. This will be my last customer, she'd told Yuri. I'm leaving for London. A few days ago I discovered that my husband's feet have grown. He wears a size forty-seven shoe now, it used to be forty-six. We grow old, we shrink, and our feet get larger. That's why you're leaving? the Russian had asked. Nora was pulling on a skin-tight black latex dress. She was in a small wood-lined room that had one of the few windows in the entire brothel that looked onto the street; there was a peephole to monitor customers' arrivals and check that they were following the rules they'd agreed upon. She opened the window and took a deep breath. She felt good. She'd stopped sniffing tyre rubber a long time ago, and today was a special day. In the apartment building across the street there were two identical terraces and two people identically occupied in the midday sun. Nora watched them as she continued to get ready, fastening a black velvet choker around her neck. The man was repotting a plant, and the woman was gathering leaves. As she watched, Nora started touching herself, she always touched herself when she dressed as a whore; dressing and undressing aroused her. It was a kind of ritual. Certain scents did it too. Maybe the customer was already there.

She hadn't looked, didn't want to, she would let the suspense build. She continued to focus on her gardening neighbours. The woman was removing detritus, pruning leaves and dead branches, collecting rubbish and putting it in black plastic bags. He was replanting an apple tree. The only easy day was yesterday. The Navy SEALs motto reverberated in Nora's mind. She had one stocking on. The feel of stockings going up her leg aroused her too. A black thong with little dangling gemstones. She'd bought a new perfume. She needed a new scent, one no one would associate with her. As she went about getting ready, she looked down at her crotch and she thought about *Kung Fu*, the TV show she'd watched as a child, with the Shaolin Master, the monastery in the young forest, the flashbacks. Martial arts and Buddhism merged, with extreme results: they walked on water. In the early stages of her conscious existence, Nora had believed that Jesus was a Buddhist monk who had suddenly showed up, and when she shared the thought with her grandfather he didn't refute the idea. So that was Jesus then, and they were the only ones who knew it.

She'd left a note on the bed asking the customer to cover his eyes with the blindfold, lie there with his arms folded, and wait. She wouldn't speak and he wasn't allowed to see her. He had to let her do whatever she chose. Through the peephole she saw that the man had arrived, her last customer, her last time. She would never whore herself again. He followed the instructions to the letter. He was attractive, about fifty, well-preserved and smartly dressed, though he appeared glum. A lot of customers were sad when they arrived. He would be the last, but he'd also been the first. Nora knew him well, though she'd stopped looking at him long ago: when you stop probing your husband's silences for hidden treasure, you're in trouble. Today's customer was her husband. This moment had been destined to happen since the day she'd caught him in the next room with that sexpot who had him eating out of her hand, the prostitute she and Maria had spied on. This would be her last customer, she'd told the Russian. Today, for the first time in ages, they would desire each other again as they hadn't done for years, or at least he would. The desire aroused by a stranger ... .

Nora didn't mind that her husband went whoring, she only regretted that she hadn't discovered sooner. What would it be like to do it with her husband as a prostitute? They had engaged in role-play where she was a whore, but this was the real deal. He'd paid good money for what they were about to do; the thought of it turned her on. Money had made her a prostitute and him a customer. Would it be better than doing it as husband and wife? Nora could understand that her husband went with prostitutes. She even thought that she'd have done the same if she were him. What she didn't know was whether Robert would forgive her when he found out she was a high-end hooker. She studied him through the peephole. There he was, motionless. What was he thinking? He'd always been good at following instructions, an obedient man. He'll make a good husband and protect you, her grandfather had told her. Protect her from what?

It's not easy to do it like a whore with your husband of more than twenty years without him recognising you, even blindfolded. It's not easy to do it with the man you've been shagging all your life and for him not to realise it's you, that the prostitute he's paid for is his wife. Nora had thought about it a lot, about identity and who we are, and how we recognise the bodies we love. The shape of things: our brains form a mental image to help us recognise them, she told herself. How will I keep him from recognising me as soon as I enter? We all have a way of moving, of approaching the other. I'm no exception. She'd been practising a different walk, another way of moving her body, her hands. A different rhythm. She'd even tried to change her breathing. She practised breathing faster, slower. How do we know who is who? How do we recognise ourselves if our eyes are closed? By our scent. Hence the new perfume. The legend of the impostor. The man and the woman on the terraces had sat down at the same time, fatigued. The apple tree was in a bigger pot, settling into the new soil, penetrating it. The woman had a satisfied look as she contemplated the plastic bags filled with dead leaves and debris.

When you've embraced the same body for years, you know intuitively the position your hands will assume. Not in a conscious way though. Most of what we do with our loved ones isn't a conscious act. Her hands would be caressing a surprisingly familiar body, yet somehow undiscovered. Robert was sure to notice something odd, something too reminiscent of something else, but it was her job to arouse him enough that he'd forget for a moment that this hooker resembled rather too much the woman he knew best: his wife. Robert and that apple tree were one and the same, they formed a complete whole.

She had thought about it on a deeper level as well, how we recognise ourselves as evolving human beings in an ever-changing world, and yet day-by-day we recreate our reality. Every morning we peer into the looking glass and decide who we are. Since childhood this had seemed miraculous to her, the great miracle of constant existence, of permanence. She looked at herself, tried to be herself without forgetting her role. We go through a daily process of securing our environment. Over the years, and with hindsight, she'd reached the conclusion that growing older was about trying to remain in the present, in a stable world, about the daily struggle of anchoring one's life, for inaction meant casting oneself adrift, and if it wasn't countered, it inevitably led to upheaval and disruptive change in all regards. Those two people, the man and the woman, were walking around their respective ter-races, circling round as they mirrored each other's rhythms, in what looked almost like a studied choreography, observing the fruits of their labour. The woman stopped to feel the ivy for a moment, and to Nora those few seconds seemed never-ending. She had just slipped on her stilettos. Whenever she climbed into her high heels Nora felt like a flamingo. Her legs wobbled and her body's weight-distribution caused a pressure between her legs that was arousing. Stiletto heels and thongs with dangly beads or pearls had always done it for Robert. And for her. She liked playing with the beads and with herself. The man on the terrace was now hugging the apple tree and breathing calmly. That little tree had been replanted somewhere else and it hadn't even noticed. It had no idea what was going on around it.

We are all vessels of information that we've accrued through our bodies, though we aren't fully aware of it. Nora had been pondering for some time how she would manage to keep Robert from recognising her. He would notice similarities, of course, too many perhaps, but she needed him to think they were just that, similarities, a coincidence, because life is full of unexpected coincidences, such as sensing that he would never encounter a prostitute more like his wife than today's high-end hooker. She'd prepared for this day over the course of a long month, over and above her work as a prostitute, which she'd long since realised was just an excuse to find herself, yet another rabbit hole, another Alice-portal ... beyond all that, she'd discovered that she was a great actress. It was a bet she'd made with herself: doing it with her husband without him recognising her until the very end. To have the best sex of their lives and for him to be dying to know who she was. Chameleon-like Nora. She'd come to realise that everything that had seemed settled, one's very foundation, could change, and that was all right, it didn't matter. Though actually, it did: what she'd discovered was that she liked that. She felt good in this new world. That was why she stayed, it was a universe where anything was possible. But, of course, when anything is possible nothing is certain, at least from an emotional perspective. She'd come to see that she was not afraid of uncertainty.

The woman and the man on the terraces had both gone back inside and slid their glass doors shut at the same time. Confined, locked indoors in their own homes after repotting an apple tree and collecting rubbish. Missions accomplished. Nora pricked the palm of her left hand with the stiletto heel on her right foot. It left a mark. She looked out at the glass doors. The empty terraces didn't seem the same as before. She rose, running her hands over her body, her latex dress, caressing her breasts, and closed the window. Time for the performance to begin. She strutted down the hall toward him. You're here, she heard him say. She moved closer, silently, her mind still on the repotted apple tree. Gardening. I hear you like it kinky, is that why you took so long? Was it part of the game? The woman removes the rubbish, the man replants and fertilises. Without saying a word Nora went over to Robert and began to undress him slowly. Despite his attempts, she wouldn't let him touch her, not yet. Your skin is so soft, he said. I need to put my hands all over your body! She started undoing his trousers, positioning herself so her thong was over his face, the pearls dangling over his lips, but Nora wouldn't allow him to bite them. When he got too close she pulled away, and then she jabbed a stiletto heel into his right shoulder to let him know he wasn't to move. Robert moaned, finding pleasure in the pain, the unfulfilled desire. She remained in control. Suddenly he froze.

She was still undressing him, but his arousal had clearly been curbed. Something had happened: he was starting to recognise that she was the prostitute. She had to prevail. The advantage of being a whore to your husband of twenty-five years is that you know how to turn him on. She placed the pearl thong over his mouth again, except this time she rammed it in, then jabbed his stomach with the stiletto heel. Robert moaned. This woman, this whore, how could she know to do that? How, if they'd never met, did she know the things that excited him most? Why did her skin and body feel so much like ...? He didn't allow himself to think about it, didn't even allow her name to surface in his mind. Nora carried on, and every time he tried to kiss her, she pulled away. She knew what he liked.

30

THE TWO ADJOINING TERRACES ARE SEPARATED BY A WALL. In one there is a woman and in the other a man. They can't see each other, they don't know of each other's existence, but they are doing the same thing. Robert, although blindfolded, had dragged Nora to the ground and was penetrating her on all fours. The woman removes detritus, the man repots, fertilises. There he is with the stunted little apple tree that's been moved from one place to another and hasn't noticed a thing. Penetration. New soil. The woman collects the trash and throws it away. After restraining himself and holding back, Robert came, and having emptied himself, he collapsed on the floor. Best sex of my life! I want to know who you are. Sure, Nora whispered as she removed his blindfold with her teeth.

She had succeeded. Robert gave a cry of anger and fear. He jumped to his feet as if he'd seen a ghost. He paced the room, staring in shock at the whore, his whore. He walked round and round the circular bed rubbing his stomach.

'What's the matter? Didn't you like it?' Nora asked, knowing full well that her husband was in shock. 'Why are you going round in circles? What's changed?'

Robert was speechless. They looked at each other; he could only hold her gaze with great difficulty. Nora would never know what went through her husband's mind during those first few moments. He paced back and forth without stopping, gesturing frantically. She followed him with her eyes, thinking she'd never seen him so lost, so out of his depth. She noticed a small tremor in his lip.

'What the hell are you doing here?'

'I'm your whore.'

'Have you gone mad? You're no whore!'

'Yes I am, and today you're my customer. The last customer of my whoring career.' She looked at him and continued to see the apple tree, she saw her girls when they were little, and the boy Robert had once been. He was scared. His upper lip was still trembling. His left eyelid appeared droopy.

'What the bloody hell are you saying?' He wanted things to be normal again, but that wasn't possible.

'So, how long?' Nora asked point blank. Silence. 'How long?' He didn't respond. 'How long!'

'Since you were pregnant with Jana.' He tried to embrace her.

'Why?' Nora asked, though she wasn't angry, and she didn't feel betrayed. She had on the day he was in the next room. Now she just wanted to understand. She stroked her husband's head while they talked. That strong man was now weak. He had just been replanted in a new pot and he didn't understand a thing. The apple tree didn't know the why of things. He didn't understand why his wife wasn't furious.

'I don't know ...' Robert's silences were long, as if long silences might resolve things. 'One day I tried it and liked it.

I thought it wasn't a big deal ... and you?' For the first time he fixed her with his gaze, no pretence, no hiding.

'Me what?' Nora said calmly.

'You ... ' He couldn't finish the sentence.

'I want you to say it.'

'Say what? For fuck's sake, Nora, why? How long have you been a prostitute?'

'Since the trip to London.'

'Since the trip to London! That's more than a year!' Robert's body stiffened and he suddenly rose, then sat back down on the bed, at a distance from Nora. 'You've been cheating on me for over a year, working as a hooker? What am I to you? Some miserable little shit! Have you lost your mind? Why?'

'I fell in love with another man.'

He was filled with rage, but there was no sign of reproach from Nora.

'He's ceased to exist now.'

'What do you mean he's ceased to exist? Nora, I don't understand! Why would you become a prostitute? What does one thing have to do with the other?'

'I'll tell you one day.'

'One day? I want to hear it now!' Again he was insisting on something he had no right to demand.

'I can't. I'm off to London, Robert. That's where my next show will be. Our meeting today was the last thing I needed to do in Barcelona.'

'What do you mean you're off to London?'

He looked scared and moved closer to her. He didn't embrace her, but took her hands and held them tightly. He held onto her hands like a child who's been dipped in the sea for the first time.

'I'm leaving, I need to do my own thing now.'

'But didn't you say the man had ceased to exist? I don't understand any of this.'

'The man doesn't exist anymore, but I do.'

'Then why are you leaving?'

'I need to breathe. We are a cheap imitation of the people we once loved. I need some distance.'

'Nora, I'm so confused.'

She put her fingers to his lips to stop him from speaking. She didn't want to hear anything else. Neither of them was wrong.

'I'm leaving now.'

'Why are you leaving? Stay. I love you. I've always loved you. Let's start over.'

'I love you too, but I don't want to start over.' She hadn't stopped caressing him. 'I've known about it for a long time. I don't want any more lies. I don't want to be trapped inside a glass case, like some display of perfect happiness, while we both seek out a life for ourselves elsewhere. I want to follow a path I can only take alone. I've always lived under the protection of two people, the men I've loved the most: you and Grandfather. It's time for me to grow up.'

'Why?' He wanted her to stay, he didn't care about the rest.

'Because that's how I feel.'

'And the girls?'

Poor Robert, he really was lost.

'They're no longer children. They have their own lives

she still needed was for her husband to accept it. That's how her life had gone, that was the hand she'd been dealt. She no longer judged anyone else either: not her suicidal father, not her mother and grandmother, both dead from a broken heart, not Robert, who went with hookers, not Nacho, who had turned her into a whore ... none of them. For the most part we all do what we can, not what we should, because if we did what we should we'd die or kill someone, or some other calamity would befall us.

'What?'

Robert let himself be caressed as his legs bounced up and down. He'd always detested his father-in-law's jerky feet. Nora's grandfather was always 'father-in-law' to him, and now there he was with his own jerky feet. That nervous tic. Maybe her grandfather had also lived a life of secrets he couldn't begin to process. Robert couldn't deal with what he'd just heard. He wasn't strong enough, he'd always known he was weak. For years he'd played the strong man because Nora liked him like that, but now the pantomime was coming to an end. All that, his own weakness ... he simply couldn't.

'Why are you crying?'

'Because you'll always be my little girl.' The look of fear and disgust was gone.

The roles had been reversed. Robert saw before him the girl he'd fallen in love with and understood that we all do what we can, she'd managed as best she could. It was over. It had all been forgotten: the fact that he'd spent half his life going with prostitutes, that Nora had fallen in love with someone else and that he didn't know she'd worked as a hooker for a year, that she was abandoning him now ... none of it mattered. He loved that woman as he'd never loved anyone, only they knew each other's miseries. She was right, for too long he hadn't loved her the way she needed to be loved, nor she him. It was fine that she had fallen in love with someone else. It was fine that he went with prostitutes. It was all fine. She would always be his little girl. He loved her. That little girl had suffered to the point of being with her grandfather because of the warmth he offered. Robert had always protected her until he forgot to … what was happening was his fault. She'd done enough by simply surviving. All that had happened, but now it was over.

'No, Robert, I'm not your little girl anymore', Nora said. 'I'm no one's little girl. I'm a woman in her forties and finally I can breathe. I haven't felt the need to smell tyre rubber for quite a while now. I don't have to anymore. I'm okay with what happened and I've enjoyed playing the whore. Do you understand? I'm no good. I'm a slut. I'm not a little girl and much less your little girl. I don't know who I am or what I am.'

They wept and embraced, licking away each other's tears. He covered her with a red woollen blanket that was on the bed. He kissed her lips and without words he told her there was no need to say anymore. He didn't need to hear anything else, there was no need to worry, whatever she did would be all right. Why had Robert suddenly changed? Because without hearing anything more he'd realised he knew it all. He'd known what was happening for a long time and had looked the other way. We all dwell on what is most convenient to us, he thought. And that woman, that little girl, what had she asked of her grandfather, what? That he love her. Yes, that's how he would explain it to himself. She needed love. He needed love too, and for twenty years he'd been going to prostitutes. They were silent, caught up in their own thoughts. Nora was remembering a conversation with her grandfather. Nora, promise me you won't suffer for love. She promised she wouldn't. If you love me I won't suffer. Promise me you'll marry a strong man. I've already found him. Who is it? Robert. Good. Robert won't make you suffer, I can tell by the way he looks at you. And promise me you'll never tell anyone about us. I promise. She realised she'd broken her promise, but it was in defence of an ulterior commitment: be yourself! Her grandfather was no longer there and she needed to be herself.

'My daughter's mother, raped by her grandfather?'

Robert was on the offensive again. He would probably grapple with what had happened for the rest of his life ... They were silent for a while. Nora was again lost in thoughts of that winter evening at Heathrow. It was as if a veil had been lifted. She'd spoken, and now she saw with new eyes. My name is Paul Smith Page, but of the two surnames only one is real, the taxi driver had said. An enigmatic sentence, but she'd chosen to ignore it. Normally she would have asked him about himself, she liked to hear other people's stories. But that afternoon she was tired, eager to get home. So the man had two surnames, and only one was his real last name. If she'd made a sketch of him, he'd have resembled the White Rabbit in *Alice in Wonderland*, but in the shape of a chubby, bald guy with a badly-trimmed moustache and fleshy hands with curly white hairs on the back. Ankles like sausages. And you're sure you're not late?! he would have said. Yes, I'm sure! I'm almost there!

'Why are you leaving me, Nora?' Robert asked again, not realising that they had abandoned each other long ago. The man who replanted the apple tree, the neighbour who removed debris. Gardening.

'I'm not leaving you.'

'Then what are you doing?' he said, defeated.

'I'm simply leaving. Someone who's kept such secrets all her life and then suddenly reveals them doesn't know who she is. I have to start over. In order to understand things sometimes you have to take a step back. If you don't have that distance you can't understand. I've never had that distance.'

They no longer needed to watch Von Sternberg's *The Blue Angel*. They silently embraced beneath the blankets. Nora fell asleep in his arms with one thought on her mind: the last time I was ever a prostitute was with my husband. When the sea is like a lake and you are doing the crawl, every underwater stroke creates, from the bubbles and movement, a shape like a bird's wing. The wing starts to form when you lift your arm out of the water and arch it forward, then push it under again, at your side, accompanying you. A bird-fish. That's what I want to be. In London, there's no sea where you can do the crawl. When you raise your arm out of the water, a curtain of droplets cascades down and is replicated beneath the surface of the water. The difference is that above water the backdrop is the air, and below it is the water. Wings, nevertheless. Touching Grandfather, being touched by him, was a feeling similar to diving underwater when the sea is calm and caressing the sand with the palms of your hands. The seabed being caressed by delicate hands, that was Grandfather's body. She should never have touched him. She needed warmth. She saw a little girl standing before a dwarf orange tree eating oranges like sweets, she picked them from the tree and bit into them without peeling them. If you always eat sweets, you never grow up.

31

SEX WITH MY HUSBAND AS A PROSTITUTE WAS MUCH BETTER than as Nora. She could understand her husband wanting to go with pricey whores. She would have done the same if she'd been him. She'd decided to leave for London because she needed to walk. Seagulls waddle along the edge of the water, pecking around for earthworms. She remembered the fishing boats returning to port with seagulls trailing behind them. She thought about Nacho and the shark they'd seen as children at the fish market in Palamós. It never happened, among other reasons because she and Nacho were never together as children. But it might have. *THE GOOD GIRL/ She's very smart/ She loves her doll/ Talks sweetly to her/ What a good little girl/ The doll loves her too/ What big eyes she has!/ It's because she would like to speak.* Satie's poem from *A Mammal's Notebook*, one of the last books Nacho had given her, accompanied Nora on her way to Segovia, that and her thoughts. She was there now, strolling the cobbled streets of that toy town that resembled so many towns in the Empordà, but on a larger scale. She'd decided that before leaving for London she'd make a quick stop in Segovia to learn the true story of the countess and her earrings. In order to understand anything in life, you have to take a step back. If you don't have enough distance you can't understand a thing. That was why she would have liked to speak. She'd have really liked that! She had always been good, too good. And one day, good girls turn bad.

She was in a bar by the stairs that go down to the old town, drinking what they call a *piedras*—whiskey on the rocks. Then she would make her way to the antiquarian that sold her earrings in search of the truth. The tables were solid wood and the waiter stared at her because there was no one else there. She rarely drank, rarely touched alcohol apart from the occasional glass of wine. I can't, I'm an addict. When the pressure of the world was too great, when she could no longer remember that the moon was a dish of milk set out for the cats, she would lie on the floor of the garage at home and smell the tyres on her husband's car. Now she couldn't say that no one had ever broken her heart. She was like her grandfather, a survivor, but she'd been hurt, and that was as it should be. The fear wasn't as overpowering as before, when she'd protected herself by working or by seeking shelter at her husband's side. For the first time since everyone had died, Nora dared to act. Nacho told her that he, too, was a survivor, and that he knew they were both hiding a secret. She had become fully herself thanks to him. He told her not to cry, the story of the Countess of Segovia was a lie, an urban legend. The legend of someone whose heart failed because it had been broken! he exclaimed half in jest. Nora knew it wasn't a lie. There is such a thing as a broken heart, it's not just poetic licence. They had kissed on the lips. She liked the way he kissed her. She hadn't seen him in months, but she was often caught in a sort of trance, reliving shared moments as if they were happening right then. Try them on. I want to see them on you. The Countess of Segovia was a real beauty, legend has it that when she wore these earrings men fell at her feet. But I sense that with you the effect will be even more powerful. Why did the countess die? She died because a man swore his undying love for her. How's that? When you love you shouldn't make promises. What? Just that. A promise weighs too heavily on love. No love can withstand vows or promises. Is love real because you love the other or because of a promise? I didn't know the heart could fail from heartbreak, but it seems it can, that's what the owner of the antique shop told me ... Nora had started to cry, the way she had that first time in the car on the way home from the airport. She was still in the bar and everything was a blur.

Since she was little she'd been fascinated by images, especially those that appear blurred when you're up close but come into focus when you move away, and by the brain's ability to decode that same image from afar but not close up. I couldn't see it, but it was love that drove me to become a whore. Then I was a prostitute in order to discover just how far I could take things. How low I could fall. I'm glad that the very last time I played the part of a whore was with my husband. A bird-fish, a bird-fish woman, that's what I want to be for the rest of my life. In London there is no sea where you can practise the crawl. When you raise your arm out of the water, a curtain of droplets cascades down, and that same curtain continues below the water. The difference is that above water the backdrop is the air, while below it is the water. These are your wings. Nora was wearing ripped jeans, bubblegum-pink flip flops and an old T-shirt. She had her countess earrings on, and after paying at the lonely bar, she strolled in the direction of Cambalache. The barman had given her directions. It wasn't far. London had a river, it would be her Checkpoint Charlie. The barman would have liked to chat, but Nora had politely ignored him.

As a child, she thought she knew what she wanted, but as she embarked on the path towards her goals that image began to fade. She wasn't fully aware of it, but the image had blurred. She'd thought it happened to everyone. Life was leading her down a different path. As Nora drew closer to her goals—a family with Robert, her painting—things became even fuzzier. But now she had a clear vision of where she wanted to go, the journey she was taking, the distance she would gain by being in London. But precisely because of this, because she saw it so clearly, she was also aware that as she began to move towards her new goal, something new was bound to happen. It always does. It is the same for all of us, frail shadows rushing along the rim of the abyss of drudgery and obligation. Haziness and clarity were not the same, they were opposites, as were distancing and coming together, though they often seemed rather too similar.

Nora was laughing uncontrollably. She had only to show her earrings to the lady at the antique shop for a box full of the same earrings to appear. Yes, they belonged to the Countess of Segovia, and women who visit the city like to have them as souvenirs. Nora didn't pose any more questions. Nor did she want to know if hers were the originals. It was fine by her. The countess had existed. The woman in the shop told her the same story she'd heard from Nacho, but this time Nora didn't weep, she laughed. You are beautiful, you look a bit like the countess. Nora continued to laugh. *Muchas gracias*, I've been told that, yes ... Then she phoned her friend; she couldn't just vanish from the face of the earth without talking to Júlia. So in this antique shop, Cambalache, they have a whole box of earrings like mine ... a true gentleman, Nacho! She'd loved him as she'd never loved anyone else, and he had felt the same for her. Poor guy, the bit about his mother had really done him in. Maybe she'd phone him from London one day to tell him that no, she didn't want him to die, of course she didn't want him to disappear, she cared about him, we all make mistakes.

To understand anything in life you have to take a step back. You need distance in order to understand. That was why she would have liked to speak. She'd always been good, too good. But one day good girls turn bad. In the conversation with her daughters she'd told them as much. Don't be good, don't be too eager to please, be yourselves, and if someone doesn't like it they can look the other way. The girls didn't say anything; they felt let down by their perfect mother. Nora's own mother never spoke again, and she eventually died of grief. Her heart gave out. Grandmother's too. Can one's heart break from grief? Yes, if you bottle everything up and never let it out in order to see where it leads you. We each have a life of our own, but we are also part of something bigger. If you can connect with that something, the pain lessens. Pain is directly proportional to your resistance to accepting it. Only by loving everything can you survive great heartbreak. That is what Nacho was doing before he found her, and what Nora was doing now. She knew that eventually something new would happen. From a distance, the picture would come into focus. Sure you're not late? I'm right on time.

32

THERE ARE MOMENTS WHEN EVERYTHING BECOMES AS SIMPLE as acting on desire. Desire is the through-line in life, the only thing that compels us to take action. It occurs when you anticipate the pleasure something will bring you. And love? Love is the practice of desire. Desire is like a pot of boiling rice, it makes those little bubbles that rise, fall and then disappear. One bubble replaces the next, and it's important to note this, because at the end of the day all bubbles resemble each other. There are men who are addicted to orgasms, not to the women with whom they achieve them. Then what? Sex was nothing to her, it wasn't important. Only desire existed. What she imagined happening, what she anticipated. She was addicted to the memory of what was yet to come, but when it came she was no longer interested. She was an addict once, now she'd decided it was time to breathe, nothing more. She had always run away from desire in order to save herself the trouble, and with Nacho she chose to stop running. My name is Paul Smith Page, but of the two surnames only one is real, that's what the cabbie had said. She was flying to London, where she planned to stay for a while and maybe do a show. She had enough savings. She'd sold her grandfather's company and divided the money into three parts, one for herself, the rest for her daughters. Robert didn't want any of it. She was thinking about her girls now, she remembered the day they'd both learned how to ride a bicycle, and one particular wave breaking on the seashore, the years when the husband she loved travelled so much she was practically a single mum, and the Mickey Mouse alarm clock going off that one morning. Two strong women now, very upset with their mother. And Papà, *què*? they had asked.

There's a hunched, white-haired man who waits at the entrance to a neighbourhood bookstore. What keeps him there? He's waiting, hoping that the woman he loves will walk in one day. He looks scruffy, a bit barmy, and yet a girl had loved him once. That happened long ago, but he's still waiting. They had told each other the truth and truth is patient, it always waits. What the white-haired man with the hunched back doesn't know is that the beautiful girl still loves him. Nora's mind had wandered back to this story her grandmother had told her when she was little, sitting on the piano bench. Long before take-off, the van that transported the luggage had turned into a Cinderella carriage, and now the flight attendant who had just smiled at her was holding a pair of glass slippers in her hand ... it was a game they'd played with her grandfather when she was a child. If you tell me a story, I'll tell you a fable. She could see Nacho at Cala dels Corbs, on the Costa Brava. He was wearing brown harem trousers, a blue shirt under a black blazer with a red collar, beige socks and black shoes, small round sunglasses. He had an iPhone and headphones. He was dancing erratically, singing. She was in the water. She had dived in naked, and as she did her bum stuck out. He watched her from the shore, she watched him from the water. The sand, the sea. He danced and laughed, smiled that smile of his with straight lips and cheerful eyes. She looked at him from afar, from the rock pool that had formed in the cove near the end of the rocks. She thought that she could love him again. She didn't want him to die, because thanks to Nacho she was alive. Maybe they weren't dead before, but neither were they alive. She had been dangerously close to joining the living dead. Where was he now? He waved his arms from side to side, jumped in the air, bobbed his head back and forth, pursed his lips as he looked at her and laughed. Laughed with those green eyes. She hadn't realised he had green eyes. She never paid attention to people's eyes. She thought about the letter.

She wasn't running away, she didn't need to now. Or maybe she was. So what? She remembered her grandfather's face. Today she'd seen his face in the sky; he was still asking her to forgive him, and she still loved him. There was nothing to forgive, nothing to be done. Forgiveness doesn't really exist. People never forgive themselves, it is always an extraneous occurrence. This would always be their secret. You must find a man who will protect you from the world. That was the mistake. To love someone is to love them when they are being true to themselves. I know who you are and I love you the way you are. Why had she stopped loving Nacho? Or why did she make herself believe she had? Why did she break things off so heartlessly? Because he'd hurt her, although thanks to him she was who she was today. Nora opened her bag and removed an envelope. It was the letter Nacho had given her the last time they met, in the art gallery, the evening she'd yelled at him and told him to leave after sharing her secret.

I don't want you to see me like this. Maybe it wouldn't be a problem for you, but it is for me. I don't like that my hands shake, or that I keep my eyes glued to the floor, that I don't know what to say and I'm unable to express myself because not even I know what I want or what I mean. My own excessive reactions, or confusing sadness with anger. I don't like that I don't know how to treat the people I love. I become a drone and treat the woman I love as well or as poorly as I treat the shop assistant, and I look like a fool. I want to believe in myself, if only a little, and right now I don't. I need to work through a lot of shit and know that I can survive alone, without you and without my mother. To face my pain for the first time, not hide from it. And in the midst of this shit, I find I'm more Hook than ever. I'm Captain Hook and I'm sailing through strange seas alone, with no crew, and if I ever encounter someone who says they don't understand me I get just as upset, go just as crazy, as when they tell me they do understand me. That's why I'm distancing myself from everything and everyone, and reinventing myself like I never have before, so I can find myself, find the monster that terrifies me, and despite the fear, kill and skin that monster. I don't need you to tell me that you love me to know that you do. I've known for a long time. Just as you know that I love you.

She started to cry. Without the proper distance you can't see things. Nacho and she were so different you could have mistaken one for the other. That's why she would have really liked to speak. She'd always been good, too good. And one day good girls turn bad. She was awakened by the flight attendant's voice announcing they would be landing shortly, and remembered the dream she'd just had. She was entering her house, and it was full of tunnels and rooms and there were people everywhere. She kept getting lost in the tunnels. A Japanese girl in a wheelchair told her that the way out was through the green door. A very narrow door. The girl said that once she opened the door she'd have to crawl because the room was full of hazy dream rabbits, some of them were a metre tall, and to get out she'd have to make it to the next door without touching any of them. If she touched the rabbits, she'd fall into a hole from which she'd never escape.

In the taxi Nora asked about Paul Smith Page. The driver was a freckled young girl with carrot-coloured hair. Nora said, Do you know a Paul Smith Page? Her question was met with silence. The redheaded taxi driver didn't reply. Finally, she said, Paul Smith Page died a year ago. He was my father. More silence. Nora didn't know whether to laugh or cry, whether she was coming or going. It was as if she understood everything and nothing at the same time. She ran hot and cold. Sometimes you only need to step away for the picture to come into focus. Of the two surnames, only one is true, added Nora by way of reply. He told you that? the redhead asked. He always said that, he liked to play with words, create a sense of mystery. He'd make comments like that that no one understood. Did you? Understand him? Nora chose not to answer, to do so would have required a lifetime.

IOLANDA BATALLÉ (CATALONIA - 1971) MIGHT WELL HAVE HAD a hundred lovers, studied literature at Berkeley, and lived on four continents. Whatever she did, a decade ago she said goodbye to all of it by writing this exceptional novel, *I'll Do Anything You Want*; winner of the Prudenci Bertrana prize (one of the most prestigious literary prizes awarded to books written in Catalan). As well as being a writer, she is also a publisher. Batallé has founded and directed several publishing imprints, has been responsible for raising international awareness of the cultural projection of her country's government, and she currently runs Ona - an emblematic bookshop in her home city; a house of culture and a house of literature. She has a son, a partner, a dog and lives in Barcelona.